Into the Thicket

Into the Thicket

H. Palmer Hall

INK
BRUSH
PRESS

ISBN 978-0-9827514-3-5
Library of Congress Control Number: 2011921898
Book design: Ashlynn Ivy

Manufactured in the United States of America

Ink Brush Press
Temple, Texas
www.inkbrushpress.com

*For Ruth Elaine Willard Aubey,
a good friend for more years than I'd like
to say.*

Acknowledgments

Some of these stories have appeared, in slightly differing versions (some in extremely different versions), in the following literary magazines:

"Blue Eyes," *descant*

"A Dead Sea Gull," *New Texas*

"A Day in the Life," *Tattoo Highway*

"Evenings on Mustang Island," *Texas Short Stories* (Browder Springs, 1997)

"Evenings with Tim," *New Texas*

"First Dance," *New Texas*

"The Home Front," *North American Review*

"Julie Cursed," *Southern Indiana Review*

"Just a Dog," *Concho River Review*

"Pastoral Interlude," *Palo Alto Review*

"Strung Out in Suburbia," *North American Review*

"The Tradition," *Flatmancrooked*

"A War Story," *Word Riot* [Also included, substantially revised, in *The Big Bridge Anthology* from Hamilton Stone Editions]

Other Books by H. Palmer Hall

The Librarian in the University: Essays on Membership in the Academic Community (with Caroline Byrd). Metuchen, NJ: Scarecrow Press, 1990.

A Measured Response. San Antonio, TX: Pecan Grove Press, 1993

From the Periphery: poems and essays. San Antonio, TX: Chili Verde Press, 1994

Deep Thicket and Still Waters. San Antonio, TX: Chili Verde Press, 1999

To Wake Again. Cleveland, OH: Pudding House Publications, 2005

Coming to Terms. Austin, TX: Plain View Press, 2007

Reflections from Pete's Pond, San Antonio, TX: Pecan Grove Press, 2007.

Foreign and Domestic. Cincinnati, OH: Turning Point, 2009.

You don't ask the meaning of the dance, you just dance.
—Joseph Campbell

The young man or woman writing today has forgotten the problems of the human heart in conflict with itself which alone can make good writing because only that is worth writing about.
—William Faulkner

CONTENTS

Mattie

A Dead Sea Gull   1
First Dance   5
Into the Thicket   11
Evenings with Tim   17
The Home Front   33
Pastoral Interlude with Two Deaths   51
For Every Season   57

Elizabeth and Others

Julie Cursed   79
An Evening on Mustang Island   83
Blue Eyes   89
Just a Dog   97
A War Story   113
A Day in the Life   115
What Art Needs   119
Strung Out in Suburbia   123

Mattie

A Dead Sea Gull

Just fifteen, Mattie Solis races down the hard, sandy beach road at Gilchrist to find her friend Todd Stidham. As she runs out onto the bridge over Roll Over Pass, a cut between the Gulf of Mexico and the bay, she stops and turns back, sees an old gull lurch along the sand, fall over and lie still.

Mattie is young, filled with life. She runs back across the bridge, hears car horns blaring in the bright early morning sun. She drops down to her knees a few feet from the gull and stares at it. Her eyes move over its neck, down to its wings. She can't see what's wrong with it. No plastic rings from six-packs have wrapped themselves around its neck, its body is clean, no tar, no sign of anything.

She feels a shadow and looks up. Todd is staring down at the gull. "What's up, Mattie?" he asks. "Where'd you find the yucky gull?"

"He's dead, Todd. I don't know why."

Todd stares out at the Gulf. Shrimp boats troll only a few hundred yards out from shore. One is culling shrimp, while deckhands toss small fish and trash snarled in the long nets overboard. Gulls scream and circle, dive into the water around the boat.

"Let's go for a swim," Todd says. "We don't have to fool around with a dead gull. They're not sanitary."

"I wonder why it died." Mattie pokes at the gull with her toe. It doesn't move. "Maybe it was just old age. My great grandmother was 97 when she died, but they said she died of kidney problems, not of old age. I don't see anything wrong with it."

"I don't know, Mattie. Let's go. I'm getting sweaty just standing here. Damn, only a week left and then back to school." Todd runs away, feet flying in the sand, down the stretch of Gilchrist leading to the ferry to Galveston and on to Houston.

Reluctantly, pulled by something even stronger than curiosity about the bird's death, Mattie looks back for a moment at the dead sea gull, then turns and runs down the beach after Todd.

Faster, he runs ahead of her a bit, leaps over logs and the flushed out detritus from passing ships and finally comes to a stop when he hears Mattie call out to him. He looks back at her. He sees her, both of them still so young, her breasts just beginning to bud, her legs already long, tanned from a summer living at the beach, his own body slender, gangly as he grows into his height.

When she catches up with him, he pulls her into the water and against him. They rise and fall in the surf and his hands rest against her hips.

"I wonder about the gull, though," she says, "why it died."

He stares down at her. His lips press briefly, clumsily, against hers.

There's nothing more. They don't do anything, not really, just stand there, touching, getting used to warm flesh. It was just a dead gull and a pair of young, young, oh, not kids, but not yet man and woman.

First Dance

They'd driven far back into the Thicket, down two-lane roads that vanished around sweeping curves between stands of hickory, beech, and loblolly pine trees so dense that all Mattie could see was a wash of bright green. Mattie was in the back seat of the old Oldsmobile, and her father drove almost as fast as the car could go. Hector Solis always wanted to see what was just around the bend, wanted to find a new bar with good music on the juke box and people who didn't know or care who he was married to or make a big deal out of it. He almost always kept a long neck Lone Star beer between his legs. In those days, the law in Texas didn't care, and he drank while he fiddled with the radio dial trying to bring in KTRM and maybe listen to Tex Ritter or, even better, Bob Wills and the Texas Playboys singing one of the old tunes.

Mattie's mother, Susie, smoked Winstons, the passenger window cracked slightly, her cigarette dangling outside to keep as much of the smoke out of the car as possible. But it didn't help all that much. Each time she pulled it back inside to take a drag, Mattie bent over to the floorboard and coughed. Her mother talked about Marlon Brando and how he'd looked in *A Streetcar Named Desire*, the way he fell to his knees in the courtyard, T-shirt ripped, his eyes smoldering with that "I want you" look, and screamed "Stella!" into a sultry night. "No one that sexy ought to be legal," she said.

"Hush for a moment. Let's listen." Bob Wills was on the radio singing, "Deep within my heart, there's a melody," and Hector Solis sang along, his voice breaking just where Bob Wills's voice broke, "a song of old San Antone." After he got religion in the Baptist church, he said his Catholic school teachers had been so mean they made him convinced not to be a Catholic anymore and he began to prefer Hank Snow and even Tennessee Ernie Ford, but in those days he still loved Wills and almost anyone who'd pick and sing Texas swing.

By the time they got about halfway between Kountze and Livingston, the Solis family would be ready to stop and have a burger and another beer or two. "Baby," Mattie's father told her, "the best damned burgers and fries are always grilled back in these little bars in the Thicket." He always said that, and he and Susie always washed them down with ice-cold beer while Mattie drank a Grapette or two. This time they stopped at a small roadhouse called Yvonne's, and Mattie almost sprained her ankle on the oyster shells that coated the little parking lot and covered the drainage pipe between the bar and the street and crunched under her feet.

Yvonne's had booths with plastic seat covers and Formica tables and a jukebox off in the corner that mostly had country and western 45s. Mattie went over to watch it work when her father stuck two quarters in and punched the numbers for ten different records. The mechanical arm reached up into the rack of 45s and pulled one out before swiveling to lay it down on the turntable. Eventually, her mother called her over to the booth to sit down while they ordered.

Her mom and dad each ordered beer, and the waitress brought a really cold Grapette to the table. That afternoon, only two other people had come into the bar, two old men who looked like they must have been in their sixties or maybe in their seventies. They sat at the counter drinking and talking about the opening of deer season next week. Every once in a while, they'd look up at Mattie's mother and kind of nod their heads. Even then Mattie knew her mom was pretty. Her elementary school PE teacher had said so when he'd seen her. "You got a real good looking momma," he'd said. Mattie'd watched his eyes move up and down her momma's body when he saw her. "What's her name?" he'd asked her.

After a few minutes, Mattie heard Hank Williams

singing "Your Cheating Heart" and her parents got up from the booth and started dancing. Hector two-stepped Susie all around the room. They danced real close when the music was slow like Hank Williams was singing that song. Mattie could tell her father was singing along, real quiet, his lips moving right in her mom's ear. Next to "San Antonio Rose" and "Honky Tonk Angels" that was his favorite song. Susie preferred the Everly Brothers, especially "Wake Up, Little Susie." But she didn't much like to dance. Mattie's father loved dancing, and he'd talk her out onto the dance floor with him whenever he could.

By the time Hank had finished singing, the burgers were on the table and Mattie knew her father was right. The juices ran down her chin, and she wiped them on her arm. There was never anything quite like burgers or even bar-b-que back in those small places in the Thicket when Mattie was growing up, and there was nothing quite like being with her mother and father when they were a little high and not quite drunk. Later in her life, she thought she'd have loved to have frozen them forever at just that moment.

They finished eating and Hector had another beer, but the jukebox kept playing and he wanted to dance some more. He grabbed Mattie's hand and pulled her out onto the floor. "Come on, Mattie baby, you're fifteen years old, closest thing to a woman in here except for your momma. 'Bout time you learned how to do this." He grabbed her right arm and pulled it around his waist and held her left hand in his. "Just move to the music, baby, feel the rhythm." He started to move, pulling her with him, Mattie's feet dragging along behind her.

The song was "Jambalaya" and after a slow lead-in, it sped up. Mattie felt her dad fling her away into a kind of strange jitterbug. "Just move in an out with the beat for now," he said and pulled her towards him and then pushed away. She couldn't help it. When he pulled her in really fast, she smashed into his stomach. He pushed her back hard, and Mattie fell into a table and knocked it over as she crashed with it down to the dirty floor.

"Maybe next year," her father laughed. Her mother pulled her up and sat her back down in the booth and finished the dance with her dad. Mattie wiped her hands on her jeans. The floor had been dirty and sticky, and when she rubbed her eyes, not quite crying, she got whatever it was on her face. She drank the last of the Grapette and, still blurry-eyed, watched them.

As Hector twirled Susie around, he kept his beer bottle in his hand and drank from it. They moved quickly, in and out, the music seeming to drive them around the floor. Mattie couldn't understand how any-one could move like they were moving. Her dad winked at her as if to say, "This is how it's done, Mattie. Some guy's going to teach you how some day."

When the tenth song played, "Running Bear," they

all went out to the car. Hector sang that "it wasn't God who made honky-tonk angels," and then dug out of the parking lot almost veering into the ditch on the other side of the highway. Her mother lit a cigarette and didn't bother to hold it out the window. "Gotta teach that girl how to dance," she said.

Mattie's father just drank and nodded. In spite of the way he loved to dig out of a parking lot, he always drove slowly when he'd had too much, and as Mattie looked out the back seat window, she could see the trunks of the trees near the road passing by and the darkness of the undergrowth. Her father stopped the car in Kountze and bought two more bottles of beer. He drank deeply as he drove and sang along with the radio all the way back to Beaumont and home.

Into the Thicket

Mattie Solis did not know exactly when she made the decision to move. She'd graduated from college and then had moved back into her parents' house. Her mother was still moping around, hadn't been the same for the past two years. Not since her father had been killed when a cement truck had crashed into the Oldsmobile out on IH-10. Mattie remembered him, too, and could hardly keep from crying at the memory. He'd always been singing some country song, always wanting to take her mom somewhere to dance.

Perhaps she'd made up her mind at some other time. She had enough money to move out and begin her own life. She wouldn't be rich, but she could get along okay. Her mother didn't want her to. "I've got plenty of room for you here, baby. You don't have to go find your own place." Mattie knew, though, that it was time.

She had already found her first real job after

11

college: with the National Forest Service making an inventory of the flora and fauna in a five thousand acre area of the Big Thicket National Preserve. Mattie's work would be part of dozens of other inventories designed to compile a register for the thicket. With her first month's salary, she made the down payment on a single-wide and talked her sometime boyfriend, Henry Duchamps, into helping her move her things.

The mobile home wasn't huge, just a living room, a small kitchenette and a bedroom, but it had enough room for her, and she had a place to put it back up on Village Creek. When she sat on the bank of the creek and listened to the sounds of the thicket that first afternoon, she tapped her feet on the cool dirt and watched a white crane dip down into the water and catch a small perch before flying off into the heavy woods.

Sitting there, she thought about her grandfather, one of the hundreds of members of the Hooks family that had lived in the Thicket since the 1840s. Her mother's father—his own mother half Cherokee—he'd grown up on the land her house sat on. He'd loved to tell her stories about bear hunting in the thicket, but now, the last of the bears had been killed off, the Thicket had been torn apart by housing developments, and only this series of parts of the thicket remained.

She'd always associated her grandfather with the land, and when he died, had wept when she found that he'd left the tiny bit of land to her. Only her family could build there under the terms of the agreement with the government when they had established the preserve, but Mattie didn't mind. Her taxes were low, and she had no intention, not ever, of selling any of the land. And no one else could build a house within a mile of hers.

When Henry had asked her why she wanted to move so far out, so far from the city, she had told him the job required that she live in the area where she worked, but that was only partly true. The National Forest Service didn't care where she lived, but living on the creek would make it easier for her to get up each morning and start the day's work.

That was true, yes, but the real reason was that she wanted freedom, not just a place to call her own, but freedom to do what she wanted to do, to walk around the place naked when she wanted to, to sit and do absolutely nothing when the spirit moved her. She wanted to immerse herself totally in the place, in the woods, the creek, in everything. And right now, the spirit moved her to do all those things at exactly the same time.

She'd had the trailer house moved to the edge of a huge oak tree to capture the shade and give her an unobstructed view of Village Creek, and the first morning, waking to a sunny sky, she had risen and walked out to the creek. She had jumped into the water naked and let it wash over her, then lay down under the branches of the oak tree and looked up at the bright green of the leaves, sun trying to break through them. She had known then that she belonged in no other place.

She knew Henry thought she was crazy. His parents owned a lumber mill and made planks for new homes and had a paper mill that turned out huge rolls of paper for newspapers.

He laughed at her as she sat naked by Village Creek and picked at her old guitar, a gift from her grandfather on her father's side of the family. The old man had brought it with him from Nueva Rosita on the Sabinas River in northern Mexico when he'd crossed the Rio Grande and moved east into Beaumont, Texas, to work in the rice plantations. She sang old songs about the slow movement of water that she had adapted to the Neches River and to Village Creek. She looked at Henry, put the guitar down, and slid backwards into the creek.

"Damn it, Mattie," he yelled. "You haven't got a lick of sense. Too cold for swimming. Too cold to be prancing around naked out here in the woods."

"Come on in, Henry. It'll wake you up!" she shouted back.

He looked at her swimming in the cold water of the creek, skin glistening like a shaved otter's. He turned and walked into her house. When she got out of the creek, he was waiting in the sunlight between the tree and the creek with a clean towel. He wrapped it around her and hugged her. "No sense at all," he murmured into her wet hair.

Mattie laughed. "Come on, Henry. When you're out here in what only passes for wild since your folks cut down so much of the rest of the Thicket, you need to get a little into the mood of things. Don't always be so, well, so sensible about everything, so reasonable." She rubbed herself with the towel and shivered.

Henry looked down at her. "That's just it, Mattie. I am reasonable. I know who I am, what I'm doing with my life." He held her more closely. "And I want you to be a part of it, not living out here in the middle of nowhere in some trailer house like some, like some—"

"Piece of trailer trash?" She pulled herself away from him and threw the towel to the ground. "Is that it? I'm not good enough? I need to change to get up to your standards?" She laughed. "Look at me! Naked as a jaybird, just another piece of trailer trash, and telling the son of Henry Duchamps and Sons Lumber and Paper Mills to get the hell off my property."

"Wait, Mattie—"

"No, Henry, you wait. I know who I am, too. Look around you. Everything you see? The tree, the creek, the whole damned Thicket! That's me! I'm where I belong, and thank God the government won't let your family rip down the trees and fill in the creeks here." She grabbed the towel and, leaving her clothes on the ground, ran into the house, slamming the door behind her.

Henry just looked at her and then got in his truck and drove away.

Evenings with Tim

Mattie Solis had lived along Village Creek for almost two years, the last one of them with Tim.

Nights, sometimes, she'd pull a lawn chair out and sit under the oak tree in her yard and look out at the slow-moving brown water making its way around the cypress knees and think, sometimes, about her mother's family and how they'd come down to Texas from Georgia and settled in the Big Thicket just as the Civil War had broken out. They didn't have any books about it, but they loved to stay up late and talk about those old stories they'd only ever heard their grandparents talk about. The Thicket always played a big part in all those stories.

When she'd been just a little girl, Mattie had especially liked hearing her great grandmother talk about the folks who'd been hiding back in the Thicket, the Collinses and the Overstreets and the Hookses, folks with last names that still lived close by, back when Captain Kaiser and his rebel soldiers had tried to burn them out to conscript them into the Confederate Army. The only things they'd flushed had been deer and bears and a few panthers. Her great grandmother called panthers "painters," but Mattie knew what she was talking about. Kaiser had bragged about how he had burned all the Jayhawkers up, but none of Mattie's older relatives could ever recall their parents saying anything about how anyone had actually died in the fires. They'd all just gone deeper back into the thicket. Kaiser's Burnout wasn't even visible anymore way back up by Doeskin Pond.

Mattie's family had always lived on the edge of the Big Thicket, and it had always been good to them. She had been the first one to go to college, and it had seemed natural to her that when she finished she would get a job working with and in the thicket. Didn't seem like much of a job to some people, inventorying the plant life growing in her section, but she loved it and wouldn't have changed jobs with anyone.

More often than not, lately, her thoughts turned, not to those old days, but to those last few nights when Tim had been so, well, just plain bad. She had been thinking about Tim a lot those evenings when she had time to sit by the creek. She had known she shouldn't let him move in, but Jesus Christ, she'd loved it. Sometimes she wished he'd be a little bit more like Henry, responsible, sober. But she knew Henry had not been right for her. Not just because his parents were wealthy but because every bit of the wildness had been kind of bred out of him. You couldn't remain a part of something when you made your money from killing it. It wasn't possible.

Tim? Tim was different. It was the liquor, she told herself. He'd come from a long line of drinkers. Some of his kin folk still lived back in holes in the thicket and even made their own. Not hardly civilized, she had known. No, not hardly. But Jesus Christ, she'd thought, that man could love her good. She still got goose bumps and a real warm feeling when she thought about him.

Some nights Mattie would close her eyes real tight and could see him plain as day and could still almost feel the trailer house shake all over again like it did when he used to jump up into the living room without even using the steps. He'd just stand there, shirt unbuttoned and hanging out over his jeans, hips sort of thrust forward like James Dean in *Rebel Without a Cause* and holding a long neck beer he'd picked up on his way back from the refinery on the other side of Beaumont. He'd smirk at her and hold the bottle just so and then she'd go all soft inside and almost melt. She knew it was wrong, knew he was bad, but she'd loved it.

It was hot out there in the summers and the creek, filled with wild ferns and lilies and all kinds of swimming things, wasn't fit to jump into just for fun. Sometimes small whirlpools would erupt in the water as big old alligator gars swirled around on the surface. But Mattie loved it all, loved the trees and the undergrowth, the water tinted reddish brown by the tannin from the pine trees, the hot, moist air and even the water bugs and snakes, mostly moccasins, that swam there.

Sometimes, she'd lie down on a blanket, close her eyes, and just listen to the woods: the trees moving against each other and the leaves rustling in the wind, a pileated woodpecker some distance off banging at a diseased tree trunk to find insects under the peeling bark, occasionally what sounded like a panther screaming in the night, and frogs and crickets and some things even she couldn't identify. But these days, she mostly thought about Tim.

Just after he'd moved in, Tim had grabbed Mattie's hand and pulled her back off into the woods, walking down the creek to try to find a place where they could wade out into the water and go skinny dipping without getting caught up in the lilies; but just past the yard, the creek slipped over the bank into a big slough. Lots of frogs and moccasins and water bugs. She'd told him that, but he still wanted to look. They'd laid down right there on the damp ground next to it. It was cool, and Mattie was warm and damn it did feel good.

Anyway, those last few nights with Tim hadn't been a picnic for Mattie. About six o'clock most afternoons, supper almost ready, she would wait in the trailer for him to come home. She never wore too much around the house. It was too hot for anything but an old house dress, and she didn't wear much of anything under it. Mattie didn't get too many visitors and most of those were kin who wouldn't care that she hadn't prettied herself up too much, and Tim said he liked her natural look and that he'd just move on into Beaumont if he wanted a woman with sticky hair and too much make-up on all the time.

* * *

One night, though, Tim walked up the steps just like other folks did and then closed the door real quick behind him. At that time, Mattie didn't think too much about it. They didn't make love that night like they normally did. They'd hardly ever missed a night the whole year they'd been together, not even when Mattie was having that time of the month, and they sometimes did it more than once. Like Tim felt he had to for some reason, but Mattie loved it. Tim wasn't quite her first, but she wasn't terribly experienced and she thought it was just natural for a man to keep on going night after night and it almost always felt good.

But that night had been different. When Mattie got Tim into the bed, he was sweating something awful and shivering a little like he was cold. She'd curled up against his back and run her hands over his hip, squeezing the bony ridge. "Let's not do it tonight," he'd said to her and rolled over on his stomach. She'd known right then something wasn't right. She rubbed her hands down his damp back, feeling the bumps on his spine and tried to talk to him, but all he'd said was "Leave me alone. There ain't nothing wrong."

Mattie felt him get up at about one in the morning and watched him open the trailer door, briefly framed buck naked in the bright moonlight. She heard the door on the old pickup creak open and then slam shut, but he didn't go anywhere.

Pulling herself out of the bed, Mattie peeked out through the small window in the kitchenette and saw Tim sitting in the lawn chair, holding a pistol in his hand, and sort of looking over it and into the creek. Every once in a while, he'd pull the gun up and point it at something way off on the other side, but he didn't shoot it. Not that first night.

The next morning Mattie fixed Tim's lunch and watched him closely as he got into the truck and rolled over the oyster shells in the drive. He didn't even wave goodbye.

* * *

After she'd had a cup of coffee, Mattie grabbed her logbook and walked out past the slough to a spot where an old tree had fallen across the creek. She was trying to be systematic in detailing the various kinds of plants growing in her sector of the thicket and was working on just a few acres on the other side of the creek from her trailer house. When she got across the log, she stuffed her papers into a hole in one of the rotting beech trees and walked back to the creek bank.

She sat there for a long time just thinking about Tim and what kind of trouble he might be in. He hadn't said anything, but Mattie could tell from the way he walked and his nervousness and the way he hadn't wanted to make love that night. And she didn't like the gun, not even a little bit. She knew the thicket could be dangerous, but not the kind of dangerous that could be held off with a pistol. Most of the crawling things would rather keep away from people than hurt them. And the people who lived there would just as soon leave each other alone as anything.

It had been different, she knew, back in the days when her great great grandparents had moved to Texas. Back then there'd been bears and big cats and lots of really dangerous men who had hidden out back in dark spots in the thicket. But not anymore, she thought. Times had changed.

That night Tim brought the gun into the house.

"What the hell do you need a gun for, Tim?" Mattie asked, but he didn't really answer. Just said something about how a man living so close to the thicket needed some protection every now and then, about how his daddy had been shot way back in the thicket and probably would have been okay if he'd had his own gun to shoot back, but he'd died instead. Tim sat down at the table with the gun in his hand and drank from the longneck and scratched at his sweaty, oily T-shirt. Mattie stood behind him and massaged his shoulders, trying to get every trace of tension out of him.

Tim didn't even go to bed that night, just sat out in the yard looking into the thicket and aiming. Mattie woke up screaming at about 2 a.m. when the pistol went off three times real quick and loud. She didn't bother to put on a night gown, just ran right out to the creek. When she got there, she saw Tim blowing on the pistol barrel like Tom Mix in one of those old western movies and staring across the dark water at something she couldn't even see.

"What'd you shoot, Tim?" she asked. She hugged herself up against him, feeling his hard muscles clenching and unclenching all up and down his body. He was wet with sweat, wet clear through, and Mattie could feel the sogginess of his shirt, he still hadn't taken it off, and even the damp waistband around his pants.

"Nothing," he said, "just aiming at an old possum." But he held her real, real tight, his face buried in her nightgown and his hands pulling her in close. "Oh, God, Mattie," he said. "Just stand here a few minutes. Don't move."

Finally, she got him out of the yard and into bed. He fell asleep immediately and was out of the house the next morning before Mattie had even woke up.

* * *

As she walked back across the old log later that day, Mattie had trouble keeping her mind on her work from worrying so much about Tim and trying to figure out what kind of a mess he was in. She walked slowly and quietly up a path coated with long pine needles. On the other side of the small hill, the path crossed a murky area where Village Creek backed up and grew stagnant. She'd been looking there off and on for a strange lacey fern that no one had sighted in the area for more than a decade.

When she reached the backwater, she slowed even more, walking so quietly nothing could hear her move. She pulled out her logbook to enter the date and time. Then spotted a tiny tuft of fern growing up from a mound of green mold that coated the damp ground, not the one she wanted, but, still, one she hadn't seen before. At the same time, she saw a huge cottonmouth water moccasin sunning itself in a cluster of cypress knees rising up from the low water.

That night, Tim didn't come home until real late. Mattie went to the door when she heard the tires crunching the shells and the squeal of the worn out brakes. He'd been drinking, she knew. She watched the dome light come on as he opened the door, but he just sat there in the pickup not doing anything. Tired of waiting, she walked down the steps and pulled open the banged up truck door.

He turned his face to her and, even in the faint amber light, she could see the blood, could smell it mixed with the sour odor of whiskey and vomit. "What happened, Tim baby? Who did this to you?" she asked. But Tim didn't say anything, just that it hurt bad and he wanted to sit there until the pain went away. "You can't do that, Tim," she'd said. "Come on inside, and I'll fix you up."

Mattie almost had to lift him out of the cab, and he leaned heavily on her shoulders as she helped him into the trailer. Every time he'd whimper, she'd stop for a minute to let him rest up. When they got inside, she made him lie down on the bed while she went to the sink and soaked a clean dish towel in cool water.

"I swear, Tim," she said. "I don't hardly know where to begin." She sat down and put his head in her lap. "We'll start here." She talked nervously, not wanting to give him time to explain. "You jerk like that, you'll only hurt yourself." She dabbed at the drying blood over his eyes and at his upper lip. He groaned and rolled to his side, but she pulled him back down flat. "Don't struggle so much, Tim. You're just like a baby."

When she'd cleaned his face, Mattie wiped his long sandy hair back over his forehead and looked down into his dark brown eyes. They were almost swollen shut and dried blood stuck the right eyelid down in the corner. She began to unbutton his shirt, stopping only when he moaned. Her hands ran over his chest, feeling for broken bones. He yelped once through gritted teeth when she kneaded the lower left rib. "Jesus, baby, I got to see. I don't think it's broken, but it's gonna be awful sore in the morning." She moved her fingers slowly, almost aimlessly, up and down over the bruised skin. Whenever she hit on a sore spot, Tim shook all over. "Tim, what is it? What's happening. This isn't like you at all."

He pulled himself slowly up on his elbows. "I'll tell you in the morning, Mattie. I just can't do it now."

When Mattie got out of bed early the next morning, Tim was still asleep. She put a pot of coffee on and then lay back down beside him, looking at him from head to toes to see if she'd missed anything the night before. Damn, he looks awful, she thought, and he'll look worse tomorrow.

When the coffee was ready, she got up, poured herself a cup and left the house. She sipped the hot coffee and stared out over the mist rising from the creek up to the tall beech trees moving slowly in the morning breeze. She knew something was dreadfully wrong. Tim wasn't violent. In the two years he'd lived with her, he'd never gotten into any fights. He could charm his way out of anything, just like he'd charmed his way into her trailer house and pants. One smile and most people couldn't get mad at him, or at least not stay mad, not long.

When she finished her coffee, Mattie walked down

to the slough and skirted around the edge of the water until she found a cluster of mullein plants with the tiny yellow flowers still blooming. Careful not to disturb the flowers, she tore several of the leaves off and walked back to the trailer.

Tim slept fitfully. The smell of boiling water filled with mullein leaves permeated the small room. She dipped a clean wash rag in the water and then sat down on the bed while it cooled down some. When it was only a little hotter than warm, Mattie fished the rag out of the pot and woke Tim up by rubbing it lightly across his forehead.

"God, Mattie, that stuff stinks," Tim said. He started to sit up, but fell back with a short scream.

"Don't move too quick," she said, wiping his face with the warm rag. "This'll make you feel a lot better." She pulled the sheet down, then soaked the rag again in the stew of leaves and rubbed it across his chest and down to the bruised ribs. "Mullein'll make the soreness go away and leech out any infection." She talked the whole time she wiped at the purpling skin over his lower rib, distracting him in the oldest way, by telling him exactly why she was doing what she was doing. When she took the coffee over to him, she asked him again what had happened.

Tim sipped at the mixture of coffee and sassafras, his lips numbing slightly. "It didn't mean nothing, Mattie," he said. "On the way home from work the other day, me and some of the other boys stopped off at Neva's bar and had a few drinks. And this young girl named Sandy came over and started flirting. I danced with her once, and she moved in too close I guess and started rubbing her hand on the back of my neck." He looked quickly up at her and smiled real big. "Hell, Mattie, I was just havin' some fun. It didn't mean nothing."

"Anyway, last night, we went back, and Sandy was there again. I took her out to the parking lot, and we were assing around a bit, just having a little fun, when this big old guy I'd never met before came up and hit me right in the stomach. Hard. I started to throw up and then he kicked me right up here above the eye. Jesus, God, it hurt. Then two other guys came up and started kicking me."

"You don't have a lick of sense, Tim. Don't know why you want to go fooling around with some girl in a bar, especially at a place like Neva's."

Mattie squeezed out the rags over the sink, then walked back to the bed. "I want that gun out of my house Tim. I don't like guns, never have."

"Hey, Mattie, come on now. It's just a gun—I need it."

"No, Tim. I'm not going to have a gun in the house. You get it out of here, today." She looked at him as he sat there, bruised, hurting, and then she turned away, ran out of the house.

That evening, she and Tim went to bed, just lying together, sleeping, waking up when she'd roll against him and he'd cry out. When she woke up the next morning, she saw Tim at the table, the gun in his hand, just sitting there.

"Thought you were going to throw that in the creek, Tim," Mattie said. "It's time. You keep out of Neva's and come on home in the evenings, you won't need a gun."

Tim looked at her, eyes half closed. "Don't tell me what to do, Mattie. I can make up my own mind, and I'm not going to throw it away." He held the gun in his hand, fingers clasping the grip. "Man has to make up his own mind about these things, Mattie."

"Not in my house, Tim," Mattie said, almost whispering.

"What you going to do, Mattie?" Tim put the gun down on the table and walked over to her, slowly, resting his hands lightly on her waist.

"Don't, Tim," Mattie said. "Just don't."

"Hey, Mattie, come on. Nothing's different between you and me." Tim smiled, held her tighter, pulled her hard against him.

"Yes, Tim, something is different. I don't believe you, don't believe you about Neva's and that Sandy girl. It's something else, Tim. I don't know what, but it's not some girl. It's been fun," she said, pushing his hands down, "but I'm tired of it, Tim. I'm tired of all of it, most of all your lying. It's time for you to be leaving."

"But, Mattie . . ." Tim leaned forward and kissed

her gently.

She could just see a weak smile on Tim's face. "No more smiles, Tim, no talk. Just get out. When I get back, Tim. I want you gone.

She walked out of the trailer house and down the trail, crossing the old log, the sun greening the whole thicket. She sat down and looked out across the stagnant slough, yellow iris blooming in the morning, opening to the sun. A frog leaped into the water. She sank down on the spongy soil and wept silently.

* * *

Sitting on the lawn chair out by the creek, Mattie smiled and looked out at the beech tree on the other bank. She had the job she loved and lived alone with the creek and the birds and the old forest that had been there since her grandparents' grandparents had first come to the thicket from Georgia to escape the Civil War.

She thought every once in a while about Tim and the way he used to kind of strut around the trailer and run stark naked out to the back yard, legs flying high, and laughing fit to kill.

Evenings with Tim had been good, but she'd had enough. No more. She'd keep to the creek and the thicket.

The Home Front

1

The natural life of the thicket fascinates Mattie Solis. She loves the knowledge that the death of just one of the great trees she lives with every day provides new forms of habitat for so many different kinds of animals. Now it's her job to think about the changes that Hurricane Rita's devastation brought to the Thicket and to document them.

Mattie sits on the edge of a lawn chair, listening to the sound of the creek as it rushes around a drifting log, to animal and bird noises, to the wind blowing the grasses and the trees. When people tell her they can't understand how she can live in all that silence, she always asks what they mean. She usually laughs, says, "It's not at all quiet. The thicket is never quiet." She tells them that when you sit very still and pay attention, you can hear the steady fall of leaves and pine needles. It all sounds like a light sprinkle of rain. You can hear squirrels racing around the trunk of a long-leaf pine and everywhere they jump, she says, you can hear something fall to the ground: leaves, pieces of bark, cones. "The thicket is noisy," she says, "you just don't notice it unless you stop and listen.

Mattie reads a letter from Peter Conroy. She had once thought she loved Peter, but that had been in 1994 when she was only eighteen years old and a sophomore in college. She looks up from the letter to watch two cardinals, vivid flashes of red against the almost too deep green of the woods on the other side of the creek. She remembers that first night they had made love. He had been inexperienced at twenty-one, shy, burrowing under the sheets. When she touched him, he had flinched, closed his eyes. She still remembers the touch, her hands sliding down his body, can feel the hard muscles of his belly, the tight skin over his hip bones. In that moment when he opened his eyes and looked at her, slid his own hand down the slope of her side and up to her hips, when she saw a slow smile grow on his lips, felt him pull her up and hold her, the muscles of his arms hot and firm against her, she had loved him.

She pushes herself out of the chair and folds up the letter. The banks of the creek are damp, cool against her bare feet. The thicket, as the sun falls behind a massive Black Walnut tree comes alive with noise—frogs, crickets, screech owls, the bubbling of the creek

—but it is not yet dark. She sits down next to a still pond, tropical night blooming water lilies slowly, but almost visibly, opening as she stares out over the water. She reads the first lines of the letter again. "We arrived in Kuwait yesterday." Iraq, she thinks, Peter's going to Iraq. She can feel the dampness of the ground seeping through her shorts, cold, uncomfortable.

He had left early the next morning. She would not have noticed if he had not stumbled against the bed. "You weren't going to say goodbye?" She had asked.

"I didn't want to wake you up. I have an early class and my books are at home." He kissed her, dry lips brushing lightly, on the forehead and left.

"Peter's in the desert now and Mattie's up the creek," she sings softly in a parody of the Mothers of Invention. Water bugs skitter across the surface of the pond. She hears the deep booming of a bull frog. In the distance a cougar screams. A cloud passes over the moon, and the darkness becomes almost physical covering her like a blanket. Cool, soft, the wetness of the earth spreads from the contact of her buttocks with the ground. She had not seen Peter for two days after that first night, and after the second visit, she had not wanted to see him ever again.

As she holds the envelope from Iraq, her fingers sliding over it, no postage, just the dry polish of the paper, she sees him again, can still not understand. When she opened the door to him, he had not come in. Instead, he had stood framed in the doorway, looking at her, his jaw clenched. She remembers that she had smiled, invited him in. But he had not crossed the threshold into her apartment. He had begun talking, not to her, but into her room, about his daddy who had been a preacher at the Primitive Baptist Church in Spurger, Texas, way back in the Thicket. He had called her names, hurt her in ways much worse than physical, each name shattering against her ears. She was a whore, he had said, a Jezebel. He had showered in water so hot his skin had hurt, but her smell remained. She remembers the way he had pointed at her, his whole hand shaking and how he had gone on and on, loud, almost shrieking, the neighbors finally pulling him away.

She cannot understand why he has written her, what he really wants from her. She slaps her thigh, feels her own blood in the splattered body of the mosquito. She walks back to the trailer house and goes in. Why would he want *me* to write, she wonders. I'm lonely, he had written. He wants to hear from her.

The letter tells so much, nothing more. Names, a litany of dead friends she does not know, different kinds of mines, ambushes, their own claymores turned back on the men who set them out, IEDs. He wants her to write to him, a love letter that he can share perhaps, a photograph. "Don't be wearing too much," she reads. He talks about Orion shining above him and how it makes him think of home and of her. "I remember how mean I was, Mattie." She remembers, too. "I don't know why. My daddy said what we did was evil. We got down on our knees and we prayed and fasted all day and all night and the next day my daddy opened the Bible and we read scriptures. I'm sorry, Mattie, for hurting you." She sprays herself with repellant and walks back outside. The thicket is alive, so noisy that no one could carry on a conversation even if there were someone there to talk to.

Write me, he had written. Forgive me, he had not quite asked. She closes her eyes, remembers the way he looked at her the first night when his hand reached out. But that night blends with the second and she hears the words again. Peter is holding her, his skin so warm against hers. They have kicked the sheets off the bed, sprawl naked in the center, her thigh between his, her breasts flat against his chest; he stands in the doorway, fully clothed, screaming at her, his hand raised, shaking. It had been so sweet, so awful.

The harsh light from the trailer frames her on the chair, the letter open in her hands. Hundreds of insects fly around the lamp. "It isn't as bad as it was," she reads. "But it's not good, Mattie. Yesterday, the Lieutenant stepped on a mine. We all heard the explosion. It ripped open his stomach. He died before the medevac even got there. I want to come home."

"No," she whispers, the expiration, soft, an almost inaudible hiss, is lost in the night. She crumples the letter, balling it tight in her hand. The creek flows by the trailer house, dividing around a snagged log, she hears the sound of the thicket at night, walks barefoot along the trail along the creek that she has walked so many times in the past seven years. Her hands clench the paper. "No."

2

Peter walks through the wide hallway in Oakland. He wears his first class uniform, the first time he has worn it since he boarded a plane for the Middle East a year earlier. Nervous, he looks around, half expects a brigade of long-haired young men and women to begin spitting at him like his father had said they'd done to him after Vietnam. From the stories he has assumed that no one soldier DEROSing from Iraq would be able to avoid a spittle bath. He's disappointed when he doesn't see any protestors. Mattie had not answered his letter. And he had taken a long time to write it, had wanted to get down all his thoughts about killing and about his friends being killed or wounded, had wanted her to remember the good things and forget about that night. Maybe, he thinks, the letter didn't get there. Maybe she still cares for me.

He is in her bed, her body molded to his, her breasts against his chest, her belly rubbing, slightly moist with sweat, against his. His hand slides down her side and up the slope of her hip. Goddamn that night was good. His father had known. His father knew everything. When Peter had come home that night, his father had taken his leather belt off and made him drop his pants and lean against the chair. No other words, no questions. "I'm twenty-one years old!" he had cried. "God doesn't care how old you are," his father had said. And then he had beaten him, the belt rising and falling against his bare bottom. Afterwards, they had knelt and prayed.

Billy died that day. They had been moving slowly down a road in Anbar Province not far from a small town. Hot, all of them sweating. Not far away, Peter could see the mountains that rose through the hazy dust and sand. No one was paying much attention. Billy was driving the lead Humvee and talking—he wasn't supposed to be talking—about a whore he'd had the night before. "You know," he said, "at that laundry down by shack city." There weren't supposed to be whores this far from Baghdad.

And then they'd all heard the popping sound. Peter swore he could see the small bomb fly into the air after Billy triggered it, saw it blow up, shards flying into Billy's stomach, neck, crotch. An IED, triggered by some raghead with a cell phone waiting until just the right moment to cause maximum damage. Billy fell off the top of the Humvee, face down on the road. Peter had watched, almost detached, as clouds of red blossomed like flowers in the streaked sand. He had taken a long drink from his canteen.

He'd written Mattie that afternoon. A short-timer, a single-digit midget, nine days and a wake-up, he wanted to go home. Billy still had 133 days left in Iraq when he triggered the mine. He'd be home first. The blood bubbled out of his belly into the garbage that lined the road and mingled with human shit, piss, other parts of Billy. Peter wanted pine trees, the slow moving water of Village Creek, Mattie. "I want to come home," he had written.

Peter feels odd in his uniform even though a few other soldiers are on the plane. Nervous, he taps his feet. When the flight attendant asks, he orders a Budweiser, drinks it quickly. He closes his eyes tight, summons a picture of Mattie Solis.

Charley Johnson had called for a medevac though Billy was obviously dead. Charley's a mean son of a bitch. Doesn't take shit from anyone. Home boy from back in Southeast Texas though they'd never met there. Peter had been thinking about Miriam, probably not her real name, a whore he'd bought just two nights earlier. Maybe the same whore Billy'd been talking about. He didn't know. He'd called her Mattie when he felt the rush between his thighs. He hadn't snapped out of it until Charley had pushed him down into the ditch beside the road. "Move, shit for brains!" he'd shouted. "Get him outta there before the chopper gets here." *Mattie*, he thinks, *Jesus Christ*.

He takes a Greyhound in Beaumont and almost wakes up as the bus pulls to a stop at the Texaco station in Jasper. He had fallen asleep almost as soon as he sat down. He jerks up, shakes pictures of Billy out of his head. The driver smiles at him, throws his cigarette to the ground. "Welcome home," he says.

3

Mattie has never liked guns, not even a little bit. She knows the thicket can be dangerous, but not with the kind of danger that can be held off with a pistol. Most of the crawling things would rather keep away from people than hurt them. And the people who live there would just as soon leave each other alone as bother with them.

It was different, she knows, back in the days when her great-great grandparents had moved to Texas. Back then there had been bears and big cats and lots of really dangerous men who had hidden out back in dark spots in the thicket. But not anymore, she thinks. Times have changed.

Peter had called the night before. She told him no, she didn't want to see him, told him she was glad he'd made it back, told him she had a new life, a boyfriend, a job. He'd begged her. "Just give me another chance."

"No."

"I'll see you later," he had said and hung up the phone.

4

As she crosses an old log over the creek, Mattie has trouble keeping her mind on her work. She knows she worries too much about Peter and what kind of a mess he is going to make for her. She knows he won't leave her alone. She walks slowly and quietly up a path coated with long pine needles. On the other side of the small hill, the path runs beside a murky area where Village Creek backs up and grows stagnant. She's been looking there off and on for a strange lacy fern no one has seen in the area for more than a decade.

When she reaches the backwater, Mattie slows even more, walking so quietly nothing can hear her move. She pulls out her logbook to enter the date and time. She sees an armadillo scoot through a titi stand and, at the same time, spots a huge diamondback rattlesnake sunning itself in a cluster of cypress knees rising up from the low water. She walks carefully around the fat snake. "Don't worry," she says. "I won't bother you."

Mattie has always felt safe back in the thicket, safe with snakes and poisonous plants, the flora and fauna she has been studying for the past years. Now she looks up frequently, keeps her ears attuned for any strange sounds. *Why did he have to come back here*, she wonders.

5

Peter knocks on the trailer's door. He's driven a borrowed car out from town to see Mattie. He wants to impress her, maybe take her to lunch. When she doesn't answer, he pushes on the door and it swings open. He walks inside, looks at the small quarters. *Not much bigger than my quarters back in the desert,* he thinks. *We can do better than this.*

He moves back outside and looks around, sits for a while in her chair, gazing out across the creek at the darkness under the trees. He knows she is out there somewhere doing whatever it is she does in the woods. He decides to wait.

Peter looks around carefully. He listens. The sounds are nothing like the desert sounds of Iraq. Nothing is the same. No bombed out buildings. No steep dunes sliding under your feet. And yet some of the insect sounds arc the same. There is an atmosphere about the place that reminds him of that patrol when Billy tripped a mine. He feels someone looking at him and turns quickly around. Nothing there.

He gets anxious, stands up and walks to the creek. Not like the Tigris he had seen in Iraq, much smaller, the flowing water is fairly clear today but is streaked with a deep brown color. He follows the small path alongside it upstream, finds the log and crosses it. He looks carefully left and right, walks slowly, his eyes running along the ground. *Like Billy was supposed to,*

43

he thinks. He looks upward at the branches of the tall trees. A squirrel races along the limb of an old beech tree and jumps to the thick, dark green leaves of a magnolia. An armadillo roots in the leaves that have blown up against the base of a loblolly pine. He aims his index finger at the armadillo. His thumb snaps shut.

As he walks quietly, as he had walked when on patrol, through a small bend in the trail, sunlight breaks through the cover and illuminates a small cypress slough. He sees her. She is leaning down on the edge of the bank looking at something. He watches as the sun glistens on her long hair. He notices the tightness of her jeans on her thighs as she bends over, sees the way her breasts fill her old checked shirt. "Mattie," he whispers.

She looks up from the small fern when she hears the whisper. She sees Peter. "I don't want to see you," she says. "Go away."

Peter sees all the green foliage, sees bamboo and titi trees, tupelos and cypress. "Mattie," he says. He lunges forward, his feet slipping down into the slough, into the rice paddy, bright sunlight blinding him after the darkness of the deeper thicket.

"No!" Mattie yells at him. "Don't move!"

But he doesn't hear her. He wades through the shallow water, bumping into cypress knees, kicking away floating limbs. He lunges closer to her. "Mattie. It's been a long time. Don't go away, Mattie. I love you."

She backs up, still on the ground, pushing with her hands. "I told you I didn't want to see you, Peter."

"But you didn't mean that. I've thought about you for years, Mattie. What we did that night."

Mattie stands up and stares at him. "Go away, Peter. I mean it."

He walks closer, his feet near the edge of the bank, the water quiet, no movement. The only sound the drop of leaves, a bird somewhere off in the distance calling. The sunlight glistens on his forehead, his eyes wide.

"I've always loved you, Mattie," he says. "Even when my father whipped me, when we were praying. In Iraq, every woman I saw was you." Peter stops for a moment, his foot slipping, throwing small clods of dark brown dirt into the still water. He stands quietly for a moment. "I didn't think you were like the others. They used to laugh at me. Even in Baghdad, the whores at the laundry. When Billy died, he talked about them. What they said about me." Peter looks down. "But that doesn't matter, now. I'm home, Mattie. We can get married."

Mattie walks carefully along the edge of the slough. She does not take her eyes off Peter. "Go home, Peter. Call me. I'll talk to you on the phone."

"No," he says. "We'll do what we want to do now."

"What I want to do, Peter, is be alone. I'm working."

Peter suddenly walks closer to her, then sits down on the damp ground that is only a few inches higher than the water of the slough. "Sit down, Mattie. Let's talk, like old times."

When Mattie remains standing, he takes her arm and pulls her down. She feels his strong hand on her arm, his leg beside hers, as she falls to the ground. "Leave me alone, Peter. I don't love you. I don't want whatever you want."

"Yes, Mattie, you do. Remember that night? I can't forget it."

He puts his arm around her, turns her to face him. "I want you, Mattie. The way we used to." He pushes his lips hard against hers. She feels his hand on her breast. "No!" she screams and pushes against him.

He grabs at her when she tries to stand up. "Just you and me, Mattie, the way God wants it."

"No you and me, Peter, no!" She kicks him hard, her foot against his chest.

"You bitch!" Peter screams. "You fucking whore!" He grabs her to pull himself up and then stumbles, pitches backward into the slough.

Mattie runs, not back towards the trailer, but deeper into the woods. She hears Peter scream.

6

Mattie runs back through the woods, circling. When she gets to her trailer, she sees Tim's truck parked beside the rental car. When she goes into the trailer, Tim is there, drinking. "What the hell are you doing here? Why aren't you at work?" she asks.

"Didn't want to today. Whose car's that in the drive?"

Mattie picks up the phone and dials the number for the sheriff's department. "It's Peter." She tells Tim. "He's come back, found me down by the cypress slough."

Tim runs back out to his truck, comes back with his pistol, "I told you you needed one of these, " he says. "No telling what that nut will do."

She talks to someone at the Sheriff's Department, tells her what's happened. "I don't want him hurt. I just want him to leave me alone."

"You know," he says, watching her as she reports what has happened. "I could have gone to Iraq, would have been real good. But I had asthma. 4-F."

She turns back to Tim after hanging up. "He's harmless, Tim, really. He's always been just a little off. And what the hell makes you think you can tell me what to do?"

Tim ignores the question. "Sure he's harmless, just another crazed Iraq War vet." He jams the pistol into the waistband of his jeans. "You're lucky you're still alive."

"No," she says. "It's not like that. He was already a little off before he ever went to Iraq. He's kind of sweet most of the time."

He opens the door to the trailer.

"What do you think you're doing?" She grabs his arm.

Tim grins at her. "Someone needs to teach the son of a bitch a lesson."

"No, Tim! The sheriff will be here soon. I just want him to leave me alone."

He pulls his arm free and walks out, closing the door firmly behind him.

7

Mattie goes out to the creek. She stares at the water as it rushes around the limb. She watches as Tim crosses the old log. She sees him pull the pistol out of his waistband and hold it out in front of him. She follows him.

Not far down the trail she stops as she sees Tim slow down. He holds the pistol higher.

"Tim, don't," she says and then jumps as he jerks on the trigger. The noise echoes through the thick trees.

"We don't want you around here, Peter," she hears Tim say. "Mattie and me, we have a good thing."

For Mattie it's like slow motion as she sees him pull the pistol up again and hears the noise of another shot and then the thicket grow quiet.

She jumps on Tim's back, grasping his arm, pulling his hand down. "You bastard! You bastard! Leave him alone. I don't want either of you here, not either of you. Is he hurt? Did you hurt him?" She pushes him away and looks down the trail.

Peter steps out from behind a thick loblolly pine. "I'm okay, Mattie. Mattie, I won't hurt you. I'd never hurt you. You know that." Peter grins crookedly. "He's not a very good shot, Mattie."

"Just both of you, both of you, leave me alone. Get out of here!" Mattie turns and runs back down the trail. "I don't need anyone!"

8

That night, Mattie sits at her table. She reads Peter's letter again. She thinks about her conversation with the sheriff's deputy. The restraining orders she's getting against both men.

When she goes outside again to sit and listen to the night sounds, she cries a little. "I don't need anyone," she says, and she believes that. She watches the leaves blowing slightly in the wind, sees their moving pattern in the shadow of the full moon weaving patterns on the surface of the creek. It can't be like this, she thinks. She hears the splashing of a gar in the water, the murmuring of insects along the bank.

Mattie undresses and walks to the bank of the creek. She dives in, not even caring if there's anything under the water and swims to the far bank. "I don't need anyone!" she shouts up into the trees. She swims back and pulls herself up on the bank and lies down on the cool dirt. She feels the water dripping down her sides. "Not anyone." She looks up at the bright moon and cries.

Pastoral Interlude with Two Deaths

Mattie had always found it difficult to talk about that moment, but as a teenager she had lost something very important to her. It had all happened fifteen years earlier and she still had problems whenever she worked in the part of the Thicket closest to Jasper and Huff Creek Road—a stretch of the old growth woods a few miles off U.S. Highway 69, not too far from where James Byrd, Jr., would be murdered a few years later. Mattie had written about it in her personal journals, not in the official logs of the fauna and flora she found as a part of her job. "When I was a quite young girl," she wrote, "I was both fortunate enough and unfortunate enough to live back in the Big Thicket of Southeast Texas, and one of my cousins, some years older than me, on my mother's side was Aubrey Hooks."

Aubrey had returned from Mississippi and Alabama before Mattie had even been born. He had grown up, grown quickly after riding on "Freedom

Buses" through those states. Three of his friends had been brutally murdered, but Mattie's diary entries were not about them. Years later, Aubrey had taught at Silsbee High School, a school that many of his and Mattie's relatives and ancestors had attended: Mattie's mother and her mother's parents and Aubrey's parents' parents, though their schoolhouse had been much smaller.

She had not really met Aubrey until the fall of 1995. Much of that summer she had spent hiking in the Big Thicket, had aimed at but not shot three whitetail deer, had caught fish to eat and found artesian springs to drink from. She had learned to live on her own in the woods for one week because she wanted to see if she could do it. Mostly, she realized now, because the boys she knew had all gone through that when they were Boy Scouts and joined the Order of the Arrow. For that week, at sixteen years old, she had lived apart from the world and in a part of the world that would permit her to forget or to ignore all of the problems Aubrey had fought against when he had been just a few years older than her, three decades earlier.

She talked a lot with him after she was old enough that he thought she could understand what he had to tell her. He was a born teacher. He told her about his days in Mississippi, hot, threatening, violent in a way that all his leanings rebelled against. He had made it all seem so real to her, and then he talked about the disappearance of his friends. "We thought they'd been burned up in the car," Aubrey said. "But there were no bodies there." She listened to her older cousin and thought about what he had to say.

"A couple of years later," he had told her, "some friends of mine and I had stopped one evening to have a late dinner at a restaurant called The Golden Arrow, and the manager wouldn't let us in because we had a young black woman with us." He stopped talking for a moment, shook his head. "We went on down the street to a restaurant called The Pig, Jr., and had a hard time getting served. I mean it was unconstitutional all over the country not to serve us, but they didn't hold much with the Constitution there. Finally, a waitress did come over and asked what we wanted. I told her coffees all around and she turned to my friend and said to her, 'I assume you want yours black with a little white cream inside, sugar?' and then walked back to the counter. It wasn't just Beaumont, though, it was pretty much like that all over the south."

Mattie put all that in her journal because Aubrey had died the spring after she graduated, and she couldn't stop thinking about him. He had still been teaching at that high school up in the thicket, still doing good work, still an advocate for all the things he believed in. He had stopped to change a flat on the shoulder of Highway 69, the road that leads from Beaumont out to Jasper, when a car swerved off the road and killed him. Hit and run. The police never found the driver or the car.

Mattie knew it wasn't deliberate murder. At least, she was pretty sure of that. But not long after that, when she was hiking in the Thicket, she fell, tripped over a root, and just stayed down on the ground, not too far from Village Creek and wept.

Sometimes, she wanted to give up. Some years after Aubrey's death, three men had offered a black man named James Byrd, Jr., a lift in their truck. They had beaten him, tied him to the back of the truck, dragged him down Huff Creek Road until his head separated from the trunk of his body. They had not even thought they had done anything wrong. Mattie thought about moving to Oregon or Washington, to places where the old forests still had a hold on people, and they didn't cut down the trees just to build new developments or out into the deserts near El Paso and Las Cruces. Sometimes, in the weeks after James Byrd's death, she took the guitar her grandfather had left her out to the creek and sat down on the always damp bank and picked and sang songs she made up herself, songs about the thicket and about the people and animals and trees that lived there. Just nonsense, she knew, but she still liked to do it.

She'd suck in a deep breath and just let the words whisper out across the water. "Only a moment, a movement on the bank / a mockingbird cries, so good, / so good, so good / just to be alive." Her words, not ordered, not rhyming, sailed down the creek. Sometimes, though, she would dig her fingers into the dirt and kick so the water splashed. "Ridin' down the highway—dead armadillos . . ." and she would cry for Aubrey, for James Byrd, Jr., whom she had never met, for her father and mother, for her aunts and uncles, for all the people she had lost, and, yes, for herself. Then she might see a white egret, sing of the immensity of its beauty, how it dipped down, splashed vivid white against the green background and she would be happy again for a few minutes.

Often, though, she would just sing her father's favorite songs, songs by Hank Williams and Willy Nelson or maybe Hank Snow, any of those Hanks or guys named Tex that sang with a kind of hiccough in their throats as they drove down two-lane blacktops in their own versions of her father's beat up, old green Oldsmobile.

Mattie Solis kicked off her shoes, walked barefoot, alone through the woods, down trails she had learned from her father and from her mother's father. She listened to the sounds of the woods, to the cries of a pileated woodpecker, the noises made by a small armadillo rooting through dead leaves. She had told Tim once that there was nothing to fear in the Thicket, no need to carry a gun. And she had been right.

For Every Season

1

Mattie Solis listened to Pete Seeger as he sang "Turn, Turn, Turn," reveling in the transience of things, in the knowledge that pains pass, that unrighteous things happen to good people. *It had not been fair*, she thought. She had not harmed anyone. She had just done her job. All day every day, she went through her section of the Thicket searching for various species of small flora and remaining on the lookout for signs of red wolves or catamounts that people kept saying continued to live in the deeper parts of the woods. She didn't believe it, but kept on looking, hoped she would see a wolf or panther.

That she had not seen such signs did not bother her. She supposed the rumors were just that and that no wolf or panther would stumble upon her. She had even found in that area a few plants that no one had seen for years. And now, she was numb. She had trouble even getting out of the trailer in the mornings and only lethargically crossed the old log that served as a bridge across Village Creek.

She thought of Tim, in jail now for seven months and getting out in just a few weeks. He wouldn't be back, she knew, but she still worried about it. She was pretty sure Peter wouldn't return either after he was released from the VA ward he was on. Tim was just bad news, but Peter hadn't ever really made it back from his war.

Mattie put her notebook down and walked slowly to the creek. As she looked into the barely moving water, she saw a flash of brown, yellow and red, the reflection of spread wings. She jerked her head up and saw a redtailed hawk, wings extended, gliding on thermals, climbing into the sky. Things can't be all that bad with such beauty still around, she thought. She took her cassette player out of her jeans pocket and undressed. She let herself fall face forward off the bank and into the water. Her morning ritual. How many mornings, she wondered, have I done this? But she did it, each morning, over and over, some cleansing rite, some way to wake up to the woods around her, inside her, to the small animals that remained in the Thicket, to the Indians who had been the first people there, to the passenger pigeons and to the ivory-billed woodpecker.

After counting to fifty, she turned on her back and continued to drift in the current, under the log bridge, down to the first turn. She pulled herself out and lay down on the grass. "For every season," she sang softly.

Mattie loved singing and some evenings took her guitar down to Blind Joe's Big Thicket Bar & Grill and sang for the customers. She got a few tips, busker's wages, but Joe didn't pay her anything. Mattie did it because she loved singing and because it sometimes got lonely in her trailer house by the creek. She thought often of her mom and dad and those drives they took on the weekends back into the Thicket, just to be driving, to be moving. She knew she was different, roots sunk into her little plot of land like the big old oak tree out front of her trailer, rooted in the ground, into the land. She'd sometimes get away from country and folk and sing a song by Janis or by Johnny Winter or J. P. Richards—they'd been there, too.

Or she'd sing one of her own songs like "Blue ain't deep enough for me" or "Somethin' happened, I don't know." And the customers there at Blind Joe's, mostly men who worked in the paper mill or in the nearby refineries, always applauded and asked to hear more of her songs or some of their old favorites, like "San Antonio Rose" or something she'd cover by Hank Williams or Tex Ritter or any of the western swing singers that used to light up the woods in the area. She'd have a beer or two, bought by some of the men in the bar, and then drive back to the creek alone.

Mattie shivered slightly with the late afternoon cool and rolled over in the grass under the cypress tree. Christmas was coming, and it was getting too cold to swim even in Southeast Texas. She walked back to her house slowly, felt the chill bumps popping out on her bare skin, her nipples growing taut from the damp chill, then ran the rest of the way to the trailer. She dried herself off quickly and wrapped up in a blanket before going back outside to see the sun set over what seemed like a million trees. Nights like this, she wanted to hibernate or just lay back in her webbed chair and look up at the sky, see the reds, violets, oranges, of the setting sun.

She was working on a new song she was going to call "Farewell to the Thicket," about the passing of the bears and panthers and the loss of the ivory-billed woodpecker. She always wrote the lyrics first and then listened to them, letting the flow of the words move into melody before she wrote them down and picked them out on her old acoustic guitar. "Ain't nothin' left but flattop pines / lumber truck roads and blackberry wine." She was humming as she listened to her own words.

Village Creek glowed golden bright in the late afternoon sun and Mattie almost nodded off as the tune developed and she listened to the voices of the woods—the leaves falling onto the ground, the insects whirring past her ears. She jerked fully awake with a start as she heard a shot that could not have been far away.

"Damn," she said out loud. "No one's supposed to be hunting anywhere around here." Mattie had gotten into the habit of talking to herself. No one else to talk with out here, she thought. She used her cell phone to call Art Baker, the park ranger responsible for her part of the thicket. She knew people weren't supposed to hunt in the area, not since it had become a federally protected area, but also knew that the folks who lived in the area, the Collinses, Hookses and others, had always treated the thicket as if it were their natural right to do whatever they wanted with it. Their parents and grandparents had hunted in the area for black bears and wild pigs, deer and duck, and a few *No Hunting* signs weren't going to stop them. Her own parents and ancestors had done the same thing. Her grandfather was famous for having killed three black bears in the same day. She was secretly kind of proud of that and ashamed all at the same time, but knew those days had passed a long time ago.

Still, it was against the law and Mattie knew it was even more than that. The thicket was still recovering from more than a century of clear cutting and over-hunting that had wiped out several species that had made the land their homes. And it was recovering from Hurricane Rita. Rita was natural, but on top of everything else, it had hurt the Thicket badly. But the people who had done the hunting and even those who had clear cut weren't bad, she knew, just wanted things not to change any more than they already had.

She also thought about James Byrd, Jr. He'd been brought up in and around the Thicket, too, and then one day, minding his own business, he'd been brutally murdered. She sang about that sometimes, too, and the men at the bar hummed along even if they didn't really hear the words or maybe didn't even agree with her take on it. She picked fast sometimes, a hiphop rhythm and almost chanted in husky whispers, the words:

> Blacktop highway
> goin' through the woods
> they dragged a living man down
> down down down
> these woods, these woods
> these woods have a dead man
> living, a dead man living
> haunting where we live.

Not good enough yet, she thought, but getting there.

That was only a few miles from where she lived, but the kind of sick men who killed James Byrd, Jr., still lived in and around the area and no amount of "we're not that kind of people around here" public statements would change that. She knew men like that lived everywhere, but southeast Texas seemed to attract more than its normal share of them. Still, though, she loved the area, cared for the people. They were her people and no matter what happened she would be a part of them, a part of that place.

Mattie picked up her notebook and walked back into the woods. She hadn't heard a second shot, and it was getting late. Already the shadows of the tall trees kept sunlight from hitting the ground, and the trail was almost as dark as it would be later that night. But she wanted to find whoever had done the shooting. He wouldn't see her unless she wanted him to, and she wanted to see who it was.

The trails she walked into the darkness of the undergrowth gave way to dim light and tall trees that waved gently above her. She knew the trails in her area, knew them all, knew each American beech tree, each magnolia, each small laurel with algae growing up its sides in dense specks of light green and yellow and spots of red-orange. In the years she'd worked in the thicket, she'd walked for miles in every direction around the house. She sat down for a moment on an old log and stared out across a cypress slough at a stand of titi trees and black cherries. It's been too hard, she thought; something's always happening. But, it had also been wonderful. She knew she could not have asked for more than to live by the creek and get paid for doing a job she would probably have done for nothing but room and board.

So, Mattie Solis, a little more than thirty years old, stood up and walked down the trail. She knew it wasn't her job, knew Art Baker would be there soon, but whoever it was might leave and then no one would be able to do anything. As the sun dropped lower in the sky, she heard whoever it was cough and knew he was not too far in front of her. She stopped and walked more carefully up the narrow trail until she got to a small clearing.

Looking out over a yellow-green field of pitcher plants and sundews, she saw a tall man wearing a flannel shirt and faded jeans. He held his shot gun barrel down toward the ground and looked nervously around. He didn't look dangerous, but she had learned that looks didn't mean a whole lot. So, she leaned against the loblolly pine and watched him.

He sat in the middle of the field, his red cap pulled down over his eyes. She saw him take a small pull from his water bottle and then stand up and look around. He turned and stared straight at the tree she hid behind. "Come on out," he said. "I'm lost, not dangerous."

"What'd you shoot at?" she shouted back and moved quickly and quietly behind a different tree. He didn't look right, out of place somehow.

"I'm new here, just started working for the newspaper. Working on a story about the Thicket after Hurricane Rita and managed to get myself lost. Didn't shoot at anything, just hoped someone would hear the shot. My name's James Bronson. Someone told me there'd been mountain lions seen in the area so I brought the gun with me just in case. I've been looking at the damage done by the hurricane." He talked a little too fast, nervously.

"It's against the law to fire a weapon in the game reserve, Mister Bronson. I don't care if you're with the Marshal's Office or the Conservancy or the *Beaumont*

Enterprise or *Kountze News*. You just put it down and walk to the other side of the clearing." She watched as he looked around nervously before laying his shotgun down next to the log he had been sitting on. After he walked to the far side of the clearing, she moved slowly out of the shadows and picked it up. She made sure there was a shell in the chamber then held it in her arm and pointed it in his general direction. "Come on back," she told him. "Not too close!"

He was tall, she saw, and slender, but she couldn't make out much more than that in the darkness. She grunted, motioned toward the path with the barrel and then followed him the fifteen minute walk back out to her drive. "Sit down and wait," she said.

Not too long after that, Art Baker drove up in his brown and green pickup. "What you been up to, Mattie?" He looked down and saw the man sitting on the ground facing away from Mattie's house, saw the way she had the shotgun loosely aimed in his direction. "Damn, Mattie. That's my job."

"Thought he might escape before you could get here. But I think he was just lost." She handed him the shotgun. "Says his name's James Bronson and he's with the newspaper. You can check that out."

"I will, Mattie, and hey, Mattie, don't do anything like this again, okay?"

She laughed. "He wouldn't have heard me if I hadn't wanted him to." She walked into her house and closed the door.

2

The next night, Mattie played late at Blind Joe's and had just finished covering three different Michael Martin Murphy cowboy songs and started a new song she'd been working on about the Alabama Coushattas coming to the area. She sang real soft, her fingers slow on the strings, almost whispering into the semi-dark club,

> "and we were home
> home in Alabama
> fished the bays
> hunted in the forests . . ."

when she looked up and saw him walk in.

> "I don't want to know
> just why you done it.
> Go back home
> leave us where we've settled."

She put the guitar down in its stand and walked over to the counter for her break.

Jim Bronson came over. "Buy you a beer for getting me unlost?"

Mattie looked up at him. Even taller than she had thought, light brown hair and dark eyes. "Art set you loose, not me. He was always way too kind for his own good."

He didn't answer. Instead, he turned away from her and walked to the juke box. He dropped a handful of coins in and punched a few buttons. Mattie watched the mechanical arm lift on the old machine and drop a record onto the turntable. A few seconds later, Jerry Jeff's "Mister Bojangles" filled the room.

She laughed. Back in some place in her mind the scene seemed so familiar she could almost remember it. Jim Bronson came back to the bar and ordered two of whatever was cold and on draft. The record finished and another dropped down. "You dance?" he asked.

Almost before she could answer, he'd pulled her out onto the small sawdust-covered floor and led her into doing the Texas Two-Step. The song was "Sixteen Candles." "Must not have changed the music on that thing since mama was a little girl." He held her lightly, and the old men sitting at their tables watched, and when the dance ended, they applauded.

Mattie sang another set of old songs her daddy had used to like and then Jim led her out to her old Honda Civic.

"I was wondering, Mattie," he said, and then stopped. "Well, we didn't get off to a great beginning. I mean what with your having to hold a gun on me and such, but Hey, I really do need to check out the damage caused by the hurricane for the newspaper and I'd appreciate it if . . ."

"If what?"

"Well, if you wouldn't mind showing me around. Art said nobody knows the place like Mattie Solis, not even him. So, if you wouldn't mind doing it, I'd appreciate it."

"I've been kind of doing that all along," she said. "I mean trying to see what Rita did to the Thicket." She looked up at him. "Not showing you around, except a little bit at the end of a shotgun. I mean I sort of assumed that was a part of my job. You look at those big old loblolly pines laying down on their sides with their roots up in the air and then look around at the new clearing and the small plants already starting to grow from getting more sunlight and, well, you can see parts of the Thicket that haven't been visible for years —small plants, flowers baked back into life by the sun." She opened the door and rolled down the window. "Come by around nine tomorrow morning."

When she got back to her home she wondered why she'd said yes.

She got up early the next morning and took her normal wake-up swim, then sat back against the old oak tree outside and listened to the creek flowing past, humming along with it, no words. That's how Jim Bronson saw her, legs curled under her, leaning back against the biggest oak tree he had ever seen, looking like she was a natural extension, some root formed into human life, in blue, cutoff jeans and a red bandana top tied around the back. He stopped where he was and stared for a moment, looked at her as she rose to her feet in one graceful move.

"Let's go" is all she said before she took off at a fast pace down the creek.

Jim Bronson followed, looked around at the tall

trees, glancing at her when he thought she wasn't looking. "This area didn't get hit so hard," she said. A few of the biggest pine trees blew over, but they were already pretty old, almost ready to topple anyway. A few of the ones that fell got hit by lightning years earlier." She talked quickly, couldn't figure out why.

She led him over to a large beech tree, its root ball taller than her. "Look. This old beech tree? Well, I suspect it's been about to topple over for years. It's mostly hollow. Rita just blew the last breath of wind that finally got it down. It was already almost dead."

Jim climbed up on the trunk of the tree and looked around. "Lot brighter up here! Come on up." He stretched his hand down to her, but she walked beside the tree until she got to the parts closer to the root ball and the ground. She climbed up and walked up to where he was standing.

Jim grinned. "Don't need any help, do you?"

She ignored him and looked around the new clearing. "People need to know that what happened here is just natural. Not like New Orleans and Katrina. We lost a lot of trees, but they'll be back and meanwhile we get more shrubbery, more natural dirt caves like at the bottom of the roots, more habitat. It's kind of like people, you know. We all, at some point, have to move on to let the young ones grow up."

"Yeah, I know." He looked at her for a moment and then went on. "You know, Mattie, this is such a strange part of Texas. Not at all like what I'm used to."

He jumped down, and Mattie jumped right behind him. "I envy you knowing this place so well. I grew up in San Antonio, but I've been all over in my work. Matagorda Island, the Christmas and Davis Mountains, lots of places, anywhere there was a story dealing with Texas and nature. Wrote about the Palo Duro Canyon for *Texas Parks and Wildlife*, about Waco for *Texas Monthly*. But this isn't like any of those places. It's so wet, damp all the time." He looked around again.

"You've got a choice," she said. "You don't have to run all over everywhere." She stared around her, motioned toward the trees. "I couldn't ever do that. You got to have a sense of home, even in places like this." She laughed and took off down the trail. "Sorry. I got to stop preaching," she said. She turned back to watch him walking more slowly, deliberately, after her. "You do that out here alone for days on end, sometimes just to hear someone's voice, even if it's your own."

Jim sat down abruptly on a thick log. "It's quiet out here, Mattie. Don't you ever get lonely?"

She shushed him, her finger over his lips, and sat beside him. "Quiet? You got to be kidding. Shhhh! Just listen. The thicket is never quiet."

Mattie sat very still, and Jim listened carefully. "Pay attention," she said. Listen."

He realized that when he wasn't making noise, he

could hear the steady fall of leaves and pine needles. It sounded to him like a light sprinkle of rain. As the sun climbed higher into the tall trees that morning, he heard two squirrels race around the trunk of a long-leaf pine and everywhere they jumped he could hear something fall to the ground: leaves, pieces of bark, cones.

"The thicket's noisy," she said. "No one notices it until they stop and listen carefully."

Jim almost whispered back. "It is, Mattie. I just hadn't noticed."

He took her hand in his, but she pulled it back.

They walked for close to fifteen miles, examined fallen trees, the large root balls, the caverns that had been revealed when the trees had fallen, spider webs, small insects, some evidence of animal life—all since the storm.

Jim Bronson acted different. He laughed a lot and seemed genuinely interested in her work. When he asked her whether she felt more compelled to do work for the Thicket or to develop her music, she said "That's crazy. I can't imagine life without both."

"There's a rightness about both of them," she said. "My granddad left me the guitar and he taught me how to pick it. I been singing back here since I was five years old and learned to wrap my hand around the neck of the guitar to make the chord changes."

"Which one's your oak?" he asked when they got back to her trailer. "Which one does a man have to rub his back against the bark of to get under your skin?"

She shivered slightly as his eyes focused on her. "Singer, tree-bound, not able to leave your own little place on earth." He cupped her chin in his hand and kept looking into her eyes. "Do you love poetry, Mattie? Are you some 'light winged Dryad of the trees' forever linked to your own oak?" He kissed her lightly, his lips barely brushing hers.

She turned abruptly and ran into her home.

3

Mattie looked around at all the people in the bar. She sat on the stool Joe always put out for her, her guitar case open on the floor in front of her. She didn't like that part of it, had all the money she needed, but knew it was expected. Some of the people who came to the bar just to hear her sing felt good being able to throw a dollar bill or a few coins into the case.

She started out with one of her favorites, covered Cohen's song about Suzanne, a woman who also knew the importance of place, not some naiad bound to the water, just a woman who knew how important place was. Then she shifted to one of her own songs and sang about the feeling of packed sand under her feet racing along the beaches at Gilchrist out on the Bolivar peninsula and about how she lived back in the woods surrounded by trees and wildlife and how

No one needs anything more

> just a cool country breeze
> some food, a roof and a door
> It's okay to be just a little bit blue
> cause ya don't need nothin'
> and nothin' needs you.

And she sang about the Thicket. "Nothin's like it used to be / nothin's ever gonna be . . ." She looked up, heard a smattering of applause and then looked back down, sang some Hank Williams, "Your Cheating Heart" and "Jambalaya," and then sequed into her daddy's old favorite, "San Antonio Rose," her voice breaking in a hiccoughing homage just where her daddy's had broken all those years ago.

She saw Jim Bronson walk in and turned to the men and women sitting in the bar. They'd been applauding loudly when she gave them the old comfortable songs. Now she sang one she'd written herself over the past couple of days.

> A woman knows just where she stands
> in the early morning when a whippoorwill
> sings
> but put her together with a sweet-talking
> man
> and the ground starts shaking, moving
> around—

Jim walked straight up to her and dropped a five dollar bill into her case. "Why don't you take a break and let's talk," he said.

"Gotta finish the set—two more songs. Sit down a

bit." She strummed a few chords and then said, "This songs for Jim, and bear with me, please, 'Honky Tonkin's' coming right after it."

Mattie strummed the guitar without singing for a full minute, picking at the string, then sang,

> You watch the mist
> you swim through the trees
> feel the damp, the dew settling in
> see the leaves unfurl in spring
> bathe, bathe in wilderness sun
> sit under an oak tree, hear it sing
> you know not to go
> know what you know
> wherever you travel
> here is all there is
> bathe, yeah, bathe in wilderness sun.

He listened, saw the old men from Jasper and Spurger and Sour Lake beating time with their boots, heard Mattie segue into another Hank Williams song. He turned, walked out to the parking lot, felt the oyster shells crunch under his shoes. He wanted to smoke though he'd stopped smoking years earlier.

Finally, Mattie came out into the parking lot. He heard her feet crunching the shells. "My granddaddy gave me some advice a long time ago," she whispered in the night. "He was talking about when he moved north across the border and headed east into the Thicket. He said, Mattie, listen. Always listen to every-thing—to your heart, to the place where you choose to stand, don't do anything without listening—to every-thing."

She rested her hand on his shoulder. "I got to go home, Jim. Got to think." She got into her car, drove away.

4

When Mattie got back to her home, she did not go to sleep. She took her blanket out, spread it under the tree and sat down. She had turned off all the lights in the house, didn't need them. No moon, but the stars were brilliant, enough light to sit, lie down, listen to the creek.

She heard Jim's car long before she saw the beams of the light bounce off the trees across the water, closed her eyes as the beams swept across her. She heard the door open. Saw only darkness as he switched the lights off, closed the car door. She heard his steps as he walked over to where she sat on the blanket.

"I'm not leaving, Mattie," he said. "You can't drive me away. Not without a fight."

He sat down beside her on the blanket, wrapped her up in his arms. "Do you always do this?" he asked. "Sit out here in the dark, even when it gets cold?"

"From time to time," she whispered. "It helps when I need to think."

"You and that big old tree, Mattie, and the creek,

too. Dryad, Naiad—whatever. I'd never ask you to leave, not unless some day you want to."

She stood up, walked down to the creek. She turned to him, said quietly, "Never going to happen." She turned her back to him, took her clothes off, and stood naked in the chill evening air. He saw her only by starlight as she slipped into the cool water.

Jim Bronson shook his head. He walked to the bank of Village Creek, and as the moon finally climbed high enough in the starlit sky that he could see her swimming, a pale ghostly form in the dark water, he took his own clothes off and followed her into the creek.

Elizabeth
and Others

Julie Cursed

Elizabeth's skin vibrates, buzzes, blossoms bright red from incessant rubbing. Her fingers dig into what must be the itch's source, but she cannot really determine even if there is an itch.

"You know how it is," she says to Matt. "You can feel your arm, just feel it. It's there, always there, but normally you don't notice it. And then you can't do a goddamned thing because you're aware of it: hanging there, fleshy, lumpy, useless. I know there's nothing really wrong with it, the tests showed nothing, but I have to consciously tell it to pick something up before it will."

The index finger of her left hand traces the fading red marks up to her elbow. "But, damn it, people don't have to tell their arms to reach, their hands to grasp."

"When did it begin?" he asks. He reaches to her, taking her right hand out of her left and into his own. A dead weight in his hand, he stretches it toward the ceiling, then exercises it at the elbow, pushing her hand towards her shoulder and drawing it back up, again and again.

"Last week," she says, oblivious to his massage. "I was in class, my off period, checking class journals and I became aware of it, my arm, big and white and lumpy. It seemed to weigh so much." She wrenches her hand out of his and buries it in her skirt.

Elizabeth thinks back to her classroom. She hears the students scream and laugh again outside her door. She hears the same obnoxious sex jokes and double entendres that have never bothered her before. As she looks down to respond to one more journal, her hand drops like a dead weight into her lap. Her pen clatters to the floor. She sees the blackboard filled with eleventh grade comments that have become meaning-less, notices the dust on the old-fashioned transom over the door, hears Julie yelling at some boy and can almost feel him flinch away in pain.

"I don't know, Matt. I had already decided I couldn't take the school much longer and now this."

"What happened, Elizabeth? At the moment this thing came over you?"

"Nothing, damn it. Nothing that hasn't happened a thousand times before. Julie cursed when some boy told her he was gay and then I simply could not read one more mindless student report."

She shakes her long hair out of her face and, looking up at him, blinking back the tears that are more painful than the fading red where she had been scratching at what was not really an itch, laughs. "I threw the rest of the goddamned journals across the room with my good hand and just sat there listening to Julie and to someone, Joe, I think, maybe Scott, explaining to her that he was gay. And do you know what Julie said?"

"Tell me."

Elizabeth couldn't help sometimes regretting that she had married a psychotherapist, but opened up anyway.

"Julie said he just needs to think himself well and he'll be cured—as if being gay is a disease. She told him she has a friend with AIDS, someone gay like him, and she talked him into not seeing a doctor or anything. If her friend dies, she said, it'll be his own fault for not willing himself well. 'Fuck doctors,' Julie said. 'Who needs them?' He said—Joe or Scott, which-ever one—he said, 'But I don't have AIDS. I'm gay, but I've never even had sex before. I'm still a virgin with both sexes.' "

"And then Julie said, yes, Julie said, 'If you're worried about it, you'll get it. You can't get sick if you develop a good mindset about yourself. But you're sick all right. Boy are you sick. With a mind like yours, the first time you do it BANG! The big A-I-D-S. You're already dead, man, and haven't found out yet because you're too goddamned stupid.' "

Elizabeth rubs her hand roughly, sits straighter in the chair, and looks up at Matt. "Is that what's wrong with my hand? Come on, Matt, you're the doctor! Do I have to think it back to normal? Is it that simple?"

"Yes, but not because of what your dear young Julie was saying. In fact you probably need to not think about it and not think it back to normal."

He bends down to her, takes both her hands gently in his and pulls her slowly to her feet. When she starts to jerk herself up, he releases her and she falls back onto the cushions.

"Don't help me," he says. He pulls again, stretching her worn muscles, pulling both arms up and around his neck. "And precious Julie's right about something else, too. Come on, let's get out of this room, for Christ's sake."

"And go where?"

"Where Julie and Joe or Scott or whatever his name is have never been, to bed, together. I'm not talking about sex. But I do want to see if you can feel anything." He draws his fingernail down her arm and laughs when he feels her shiver.

"So someone told Julie he was gay," he says.

"And Julie cursed," she whispers.

As they walk into the bedroom, she squeezes his neck, mock ferociously, with both hands, leans into him comfortably, her hip against his, and whispers close to his ear, "It's all right, isn't it, not to like them, at least not all the time?"

An Evening on Mustang Island

The salt water, clear even in the dark, but speckled with small tar balls, the residue of an oil well blow-out in the Bay of Campeche years earlier, washed over Elizabeth's bare feet. She stood, silent, holding Matt's hand lightly. Looking out at the oil rigs, platforms lit up like small towns in the darkness, she felt the tepid water around her ankles, felt the sand sliding, seeming to slip away under her.

"What are you thinking about, Matt?" she broke the silence, not seeing his face clearly in the moonless night, sensing that his mood had shifted.

"What I always think about the first night we're here." She watched Matt look out into the surf washing the debris onto the shores of Mustang Island. "Dad was fifty years old," she heard him say, "would have been eighty this year, barring heart attacks or cancer."

Elizabeth had heard this same speech, about the shock, about the problem of not knowing, many times.

Each time they came to the coast. Her mind drifted as she listened; her fingers drew meaningless lines in the damp sand. "The ship simply vanished," he had told her. "Seven days out from port."

As he talked, Elizabeth grew more uncomfortable. She and the children, now grown, one in college, the other married, had heard the story so often, they could almost speak it with him. She understood, she thought, why he had to tell it so often. Not "Ancient Mariner" stuff, but still some compulsion to keep his father alive. He should let him die, she thought.

"It's so strange, Elizabeth."
She blinked her eyes in rhythm with the pulsing of a bright red light glowing just above the horizon.

"All those years, all those ships, and the Queen was the only one I had ever actually stepped on. I carried my father's suitcase into his cabin. I remember telling him I thought it was awfully small for someone whose title was First Officer. His cabin was maybe eight feet by six feet, just enough room for the cot, welded to the floor, and a small table. The deck was gray, slippery, and the whole ship smelled of sulphur, like rotten eggs, but more pungent."

Elizabeth smiled, knowing Matt wouldn't see, but knowing, too, that it would lighten her voice. She had heard the story so many times. The first night at the coast, the sound of the surf rolling onto the island, the view of the lights bouncing off the water, always took Matt back to that night in 1963, built up the words in an almost set piece that he released in a low, slowly rhythmic monotone. "Let's sit down, Matt, here in the sand, by the water."

As she sat in the damp sand, Matt lit a cigarette. In the flare of the match, she saw the tension in his face, his jaws working, his eyes staring out at the dark horizon. She waited for the rest of the speech.

She saw him inhale deeply and let the harsh smoke slowly out into the salty air. As he knelt down facing her, facing the sea, she thought about the few changes she could notice since they had bought the beach house ten years earlier. A little more weight, not much; his knees made quiet popping sounds as he knelt in front of her, but the motion was effortless; his hair was thinner. She had not changed much more, she knew. Oh, there was less tone to her muscles and some gray, now, in her hair. Matt had wanted her to put a rinse on it, but she would not. He had backed off quickly when she asked if he found her less attractive now that she was well into middle age.

She knew he had almost worked the story out. The beat picked up, his voice grew slightly louder. The monotonous tone found variety. She tuned him out, not listening to anything but the cadence, nodding from time to time.

"I'm sorry, Elizabeth," he said. "It must bore you. Every time we come to the beach, I blather on about it. But there's something about the place. Dad always wanted a beach house, but we could never afford one."

Elizabeth clasped Matt's hand tighter. Over his shoulders, she could see the dark waters and the moon just beginning to rise behind the rigs.

The red lights blinked with infuriating regularity, and she heard a ship sounding its deep horn to signal its intention of moving between the jetties and into the pass leading through the intracoastal canal to Corpus Christi.

She sensed, rather than saw, Matt bury his cigarette in the sand, felt his quick kiss, tasted the salt air and grit of the beach on his lips, watched him stand up and run out into the surf. She breathed faster as she saw his body arch, his legs kick up. He dove into the waves cresting over the first sandbar and swam with deliberate strokes, as if to the metronome that marked the cadence of his father's death story, beyond the second. As she watched, her eyes focused on the slim whiteness of his body moving out in the direction of the shining rigs.

"Matt!" she screamed. "Matt! Come back!" She lost sight of him as rows of dark swells blotted him from view.

Elizabeth waded out into the surf. When she reached the first sandbar, she stood and looked out toward the blinking lights. She was not a good swimmer, had always been afraid of the night waters of the Gulf of Mexico. She hesitated on the shallow sand and then, still unable to see him, waded farther out.

When the water rose above her head, she dog

paddled slowly toward the next barrier of sand, toward the second row of white-in-the-moonlight breakers. There the water came only to her waist and she could stand on her own, jumping high as the waves lifted her from her feet.

"Matt," she whispered quietly into the approaching waves, coughing the salt water out of her mouth. "Matt! Where are you?"

A large wave rose above her and the immense force of its undertow pulled her farther out, plunged her down into the water, scraped her arm as it rolled her along the sandy bottom. Under the dark water, she sensed motion. Opening her eyes to the burning salt, she saw a vaguely white shape moving swiftly toward her. Her feet once more on the sand, she backed frantically away, and then felt something pushing her upward, grabbing her and pulling her down. She shrieked, jerked away, turned back towards shore. And then, her heart beating faster, relaxed as Matt's arms and a towering wave lifted her gently toward the sky.

"You son of a bitch," she laughed, then cried. "I thought you had drowned " Holding his head, she felt the wet coarseness of his hair from the salty water, looked into his dark eyes in the moonlight and saw the depth that had always been there, the pain not quite washed away. "Don't ever, ever do anything like that again, Matt. Not ever again."

"Did it frighten you that much? I thought you were used to the ocean, would know that—"

87

"Of course I was frightened, damn it. You know I hate the ocean at night. But that's not all. All that talk, Matt. Your father and his godforsaken ship. Stop it! Just stop. I thought you'd decided to just keep swimming until you no longer had the strength to return."

"That was a long time ago, Elizabeth," he said, "more than half a lifetime. I'd still like to know what happened. I just needed to swim, to spend energy, to dive as deeply as I could."

His arms pulled her closer, and they stood there for several minutes, holding each other, rising and falling with the waves, washed in warm water.

Blue Eyes

I had never seen them before. Not here at LouAnn's Country Store, a combination restaurant and dance hall where five-piece bands come to play their own renditions of Hank Williams and Waylon Jennings, with a little nod to Willie Nelson every once in a while. A little nod? I don't think I've ever been to The Store without hearing "Blue Eyes Crying in the Rain." I'm often the only person here alone and I don't mind that even a little. Enough women ask me to dance that I always have a good time. That's the nice thing about being a regular. Hell, a few even invite me back to their houses after LouAnn's closes. And I usually go. It's all just for fun. But it's not really that kind of a place. I mean families bring their kids here to eat and dance to Texas swing. When "Cotton-Eyed Joe" gets going, even the little kids get in line and kick and step out, better'n most of the grown ups.

But I was talking about them. The young man and

woman I hadn't ever seen here before. He looked kind of slicked back, if you know what I mean. He'd combed his stringy blond hair back and plastered it down to his head. Real good looking and I thought most women would have liked him a lot. But he had kind of a "don't trust me" look that he hid behind a smile. She was taller than him, a little on the skinny side, even better looking than him. She seemed pretty pale, though, sitting across from him at the table. She wore a man's white dress shirt over faded almost white jeans and had sandals on her feet. His shirt was deep and sparkling blue, covered with sequins like so many fake cowboy shirts are. He wore boots that shone almost as much as the sequins. And I could see they weren't very happy.

I shouldn't have been looking at them so much, but I didn't think they'd notice. He was smoking, tapping his fingers on the table, and they were talking very low. I doubt that anyone could hear them, not even if they were sitting at the booth just behind them. She looked at him with a real intense look. Every once in a while she'd brush the hair out of her eyes, but her hair wasn't always in her eyes when she did it and I knew she was crying a little. Just as I was getting real curious about why she was crying and why he was puffing so hard on his cigarette, Ruth Pollard stopped by my table.

"I've always loved 'Eatin' My Heart Out Over You,' Bud. Come dance with me, okay?" I nodded and stood up just as The Crooked Horseshoe sang, ". . . and there ain't nothing left for dessert."

Ruthie was the kind of woman who liked to lead. A big woman—when you put your arms around her you knew you had your arms around something that could just run away with you and you wouldn't be able to stop it. She held me real close and sang softly in my ear, "My husband's eatin' me outta house and home / while I eat my heart out over you."

It wasn't one of my favorite songs and The Horseshoe weren't even doing a very good job of it. But Ruthie seemed to be enjoying it. I finally got a good hold on her and steered her across the floor near the young couple I'd developed some kind of an interest in. But even dancing right next to them, with Ruthie's hips endangering their table, I couldn't hear what they were saying. I did notice that the woman was dabbing at her eyes with her napkin.

Ruthie managed to get me back under control, and her rather large bosom herded me back into the middle of the floor. When the band stopped playing that wretched song and segued into "I Cried a River Over you," I excused myself on the grounds of needing another Shiner Bock and walked back to my table.

My fascination with that young couple did not abate in any way. The band whipped into a few bars of "All My Exes Live in Texas, and that's why I hang my hat in Tennessee" just as she covered her face with her hands, and I became convinced that he had brought

91

her out to LouAnn's just to tell her that he wanted a divorce. It's a good way to do it. Not that I've ever done anything like that. But if I was married and was going to ask my wife for a divorce, I suspect a public place might be pretty appealing.

It's a little tarnished, with a few chips broken off, but LouAnn's has one of those big old mirrored balls that turns and sends things that look like little stars spinning around the room. I've always kind of enjoyed that even though it's become a real low class kind of thing lately. Anyway, just as she stood up to go the bathroom or something, one of the little reflections raced across her eyes, and I could tell she'd been crying pretty good. Maybe it wasn't a divorce. Maybe she was pregnant and the son of a bitch wouldn't marry her. Could be almost anything.

"Hey, Bud, whatcha thinkin' 'bout?" Shit. Mary Alice Guidry. She and I'd had a thing going for a while and she hadn't been too happy when I broke it off. "I'd like to say I was thinking about you, Mary Alice, but to be honest my mind was just a total blank. Must be the music." I looked up at her. She was wearing one of those low cut dresses she always liked to show herself off in, but gravity was just starting to make itself known. "Didn't say whether it's good or bad, now did I?" Mary Alice's husband owned LouAnn's. It was named after his first wife, and I figured she'd tell him a good customer didn't much like tonight's band.

"Come dance with me, cowboy," she said. And I

had to confess, though she already knew it, that I wasn't a cowboy. Big accounting firms don't really have much use for cowboys.

I couldn't help laughing when the band started up on a few choruses of "Long Tall Texan." You know the song, I'm sure. Everyone who's spent much time in a Texas bar knows it.

> Well, I'm a long tall Texan
> I got a girl named Sue . . .

And it goes through about a hundred girls' names telling what they do so special before the song ends. They sang one about

> a girl named Mary
> and when you get real close, boys,
> it's like front row at the dairy.

My favorite verse was always about a girl named Jean, but the lyric and her both weren't very

> clean,
> —if you know what I mean
> Huh- hu-huh-hu-huh-hu-huh-hu!

so they couldn't sing it in a place like this.

Mary Alice was the kind of woman that when you danced with her she was like a part of you, her thighs against yours, her belly rubbing against you, her breasts in perpetual motion, and she liked to try to scoot your hand down to rest on her bottom. I guess you can see why we had that little thing not too long ago.

Anyway, I talked old Mary Alice into going into the

bathroom and seeing if that young woman needed any help. When she came back, she told me the only woman in the bathroom was sitting in one of the stalls behind a door, and she just couldn't think of any way to bang on the thing and say, "Need any help, hon?" "Wouldn't seem just right, you know?" So she grabbed me again and relaxed all over me while the band sang "Don't Get Around Much Anymore."

I really shouldn't have let myself get interested in that little girl. I danced a few more times and overheard a word or two, but I never did find out what was wrong with her. Except I was pretty sure it was the man she was with. He was no good, I could tell by looking, but some women like men like that.

Hell, look at all those movie stars and musicians and the women who chase after them. I mean even big old ugly men who can't really sing very well and those big old Wrestlers like Gorgeous George who used to grease up their bodies or something, they have to fight women off with a stick sometimes. And this guy wasn't even ugly.

I was already walking over to ask her to dance when the band started up on "Blue Eyes Crying in the Rain," and when I got a few feet from their table they both stood up. She looked right at me, kind of cold like, blue eyes in a hard face. Anyway, she turned to the guy she was with and told him to sit back down again. "I want to dance with this guy; he's been lookin' at me all night," she told him. He nodded and sat back down.

She put one hand in mine and the other back behind my neck and I danced her around the sawdust dance floor a few times. But it was almost like she wasn't there. I asked her what her name was and she didn't say anything. I asked her if she was okay, why she'd been crying and if she needed any help. She hummed along a little with the song, but didn't say a single word. The whole time we were dancing, she kept her body at least three inches away from mine and looked right in my eyes. Maybe not in my eyes, but through them, like she wasn't really seeing anything. I can't recall seeing her blink even once. And when the boys finally sang, "In a world that knows no part of / blue eyes cryin' in the rain," she took her arms away from me and ran out of LouAnn's with that guy racing after her.

Me? I went back to my table and then out back with Mary Alice. Hell, I'd have gone with Ruthie if she hadn't already headed home.

Just a Dog

always hate it when that sort of thing happens. I'd been driving down the road and suddenly a bird, a stupid dove, what else, white-tipped wings a blur, flew right in front of my car. Next thing I knew, wham, a bigassed dog smacked into me, hitting so hard my windshield cracked. I heard this quick, shrill yelp and saw this stupid dog fly at least ten feet into the air. It all happened suddenly, but I saw it real slow, like a film in slow motion. Five minutes later, I could still see the dog's image, some kind of fancy dog, not a mutt. And then I felt guilty as hell.

If I hadn't been in such a hurry to get to the Blue Star Art Space, I would have stopped. But I didn't see how I could do anything to help the dog, I mean he was dead, doomed anyway, and I could see all right through the broken windshield and, besides, I didn't want to be late again.

My girlfriend, Margaret Ellis, was fidgeting over

her first major exhibit and expected me to be there to give her moral support and maybe afterwards, if things went right, a little immoral comfort. I felt bad about the damned dog, though. I would have stopped except I knew how ticked off Margaret would be if I showed up even a few minutes late.

All that evening, I kept seeing the dog bouncing off my windshield. Frozen in mid-jump, a white-tipped dove just out of reach. The dog, his tongue out, glared at me even through the great swirls and gobs of reds and blues on gray in Margaret's paintings. I laughed, very quietly I thought, reminded for a moment of the lovers my old English teachers had talked about on Keats's Grecian urn. *He'd been a fine looking dog, though, could really jump.* I drove a Bronco II, not some little Miata kind of a car. It took a real jump for the dog to hit the windshield.

"You look lost in thought, Paul." Margaret handed me a glass of wine and a toothpick with a small cube of cheese. "What's so funny? You don't like this painting?"

"Just thinking about a dead dog, Margaret."

"Glad you're not an art critic!" Margaret frowned and hit me in the stomach, hard, then let the palm of her hand rest there for a moment. "Think it's going okay?"

"Hell, babe, you know it is. They love you." I slipped my arm around her waist and pulled her against my hip.

Slightly hung over, my head throbbing, I left Margaret's house early the next morning. Driving slowly back to my own place, each bump in San Pedro Avenue causing my head to throb, I saw a man standing in front of the closest house to the spot in the road where I'd hit the dog. I let the Bronco roll to a stop and walked over to him. "Just wanted to tell you how sorry I am about what happened yesterday afternoon," I said. But he didn't say anything back. "I mean about the dog and all. If he was your dog."

"Yeah," he said. "The dog was mine. I recognized your pickup."

"You're not from around here, are you?" Not quite as young as I had initially thought, he was one of those men who blew their hair dry so it would poof up and cover most of the thin spots. Yeah, folks from around here did that, but no real Texan would call a Bronco II a pickup.

"No, we're not from here."

"Where you from?" I asked. "My name's Paul Broller. Been living in the neighborhood for about ten years."

He kept on staring out at the road and not talking, just kind of looking at nothing, until I finally decided I'd had enough of the silence and started to walk back to the car.

"Cleveland," he said, "Ohio," like he thought I wouldn't know where Cleveland was unless he told me. You know how some of those Midwesterners can be. "My name's Johnson. Wait here a minute. No, come on in. Maybe, you can explain the damn dog to her."

The house looked like all the other houses in the neighborhood: saltillo tile in the entry bumped against beige carpeting on the floors. What art hung on the walls was mostly decent prints, impressionists and cubists, a pale imitation of Van Gogh's sunflowers, Picasso's "Man with a Blue Guitar," that sort of thing. *Really gettin' to be an arts snob since Margaret, aren't you?* I grinned. I hadn't known a damned thing about art until I'd started sleeping with my own art dictionary.

Johnson's wife sat at the counter where the kitchen overlooked the breakfast room. I smiled automatically when I saw her, a good-looking woman. Thin, with short black hair curled under, evenly, all around her head, she had a long, aquiline neck, that the undercurl of her hair accented. Pretty, but almost artificially so, kind of like the prints hanging on the walls. She deliberately opened her eyes wide before looking directly into mine. You know how some women can do that, just pull something up from about surface deep and their eyes widen all of a sudden?

"Who are you?" Her voice was husky like she'd been crying a lot.

"He's the man who killed Sebastian," Johnson said.

"Well," I said, smiling, still looking directly into her

eyes, a staring contest like I used to have with my older brother when I was a kid, but not really happy with the way I'd been introduced, "not quite, Ms. Johnson. But I am the man against whose car Sebastian committed suicide, assuming Sebastian was the name of your dog." I cleared my throat. "My name's Paul Broller, and I live up the road a bit from you."

She didn't even blink. "That wasn't very funny, Mr. Broller," she said.

"Perhaps not, ma'am, but it's true. Don't believe I caught your name?"

"We should never have moved to San Antonio, Robert," she said. I assumed that was Johnson's first name since he was the only other person in the room. "It's not a civilized place."

I couldn't help smiling, choked back a laugh. "Like Cleveland?"

"Yes, like Cleveland. Cleveland's wonderful, civilized, not some silly town that sprang up overnight like all these cowboy places."

I stuck my thumbs between the thick leather of my belt and the rough denim, thrusting my hips forward slightly. I couldn't help myself, played out the cowboy role a bit. If I'd had a rope I would have fiddled with it, even though I'd never roped a steer in my life. I sometimes overdo it when people act like that. "People been living and loving and playing good music here since Cleveland wasn't even thought about, ma'am," I said. But she didn't seem to hear me.

Her eyes turned from mine, followed my hands and focused on the silver belt buckle Margaret had given me, an engraved seahorse pointed upside down. "We should never have moved to Texas."

"That may be ma'am, but I just came by to say how sorry I am about your dog. Guess I'd better leave you folks alone." When I turned around and started back out to the front door, Johnson grabbed my right arm and squeezed it.

"That dog cost $640," the man said. "Who's going to pay for it?"

"I suppose you folks are." I gently, but firmly, pulled his hand off my arm, squeezing it tight. Had no idea why these people brought out that kind of play in me. "If you want to replace him. Lots of money to pay for a dog, though, when you can get one at the shelter for only twenty-five bucks. That's where I got both of mine."

"I'd like to see your driver's license, please," Johnson said, "to bill you for the cost of Sebastian."

I drew back for a moment, kinda smiled at him to keep from answering too loudly. "Let me see yours, Mr. Johnson."

"Why do you need to see mine?"

"Gotta give it to the insurance company. Your damned dog broke my windshield and then put a little dent in my hood. Must be seven or eight hundred bucks worth of damage." I propped my foot up on the arm of one of Ms. Johnson's chairs and dropped my fingers back over my belt buckle. "Tell you what. I'll skip the windshield. My own insurance'll pay for that."

"That's an interesting belt buckle, Mr. Broller," the woman said. "Why's the seahorse upside down?"

"As soon as your husband and I come to terms, ma'am, I'll tell you all about it." I turned back to Johnson. "We got an ordinance in San Antonio, Mr. Johnson. Says you've got to keep your dog on a leash or in a fenced-in yard. I don't like running over dogs, but your damned dog leaped right up against my windshield while he was chasing a bird. You had a fence, he'd still be here."

"Let it go, Robert," she said. "Mr. Broller must know much more about this kind of place than we ever could. We'll just have to get another dog." She looked at me as if I were one of the exhibits down at the Blue Star: 'Tall Texan with Belt Buckle.' "Now tell me about that upside down seahorse, Mr. Broller."

"Paul, ma'am. There's really not much to tell. Just a gift from a girlfriend. Seahorse is upside down 'cause she tried the belt on herself just to see how it would look and it looked fine. She didn't think about how men put their belts on backwards from women." I stopped talking and looked at her carefully. She seemed to be listening but had that sophisticated way of not appearing to pay attention. "Anyway, I like the damned thing, even upside down."

Everything went real quiet for a minute. Then Johnson said something like it didn't seem we were getting anywhere and I agreed with him and apologized again about their dog. Ms. Johnson said to forget about it and stood up. "Not the nicest way to meet a new neighbor, Mr. Broller," she said and held her hand out in that kind of prissy, stuck up way some women have, making her hand real small and bending at the wrist. Margaret had a good handshake, strong and direct. When I took Ms. Johnson's in mine, it was just kind of there, no pressure, nothing.

Margaret dragged me out to another art opening in October, this one at a gallery on the north side of town, near the Medical Center. The work wasn't anything like hers. I bought a painting of a little toy boat being pulled through water running down a ditch, grass blades bright and dark green on either side, a string held by a kid you couldn't see anything of except his hand kept the little white boat in the center of the stream.

She stood behind me. I thought it was Margaret for a moment, didn't really see who it was as I finished paying the gallery owner. It wasn't until I turned around and brushed against her that I realized it was the Johnson woman, the one with the dog. She looked embarrassed for a moment, then smiled and held out her hand. "I didn't know you were a collector, Mr. Broller."

I covered her hand with mine, squeezing it a bit like I was shaking hands with a human being, and looked her in the eyes. She was dressed in clothes that might have been appropriate for Cleveland in October, but couldn't have been too comfortable that night. Her hair didn't seem to be affected, though. Still perfect, that little curl under that accented her neck. "I'm not really a collector. Just buy a few things when I like them."

"And you like this?"

"Romo's boat? Yes, ma'am. It's real fine. The colors, the sharp edges. Margaret calls it 'practiced primitivism.' It's kind of raw and emotional. You have to see some of the paintings by Ito and some of the other Chicano painters around here to know what's vital in this whole area." I stopped, embarrassed a little. "Didn't mean to start a lecture, Ms. Johnson."

"It's Judith, Mr. Broller. We don't get out much with all the shootings and stuff, but this isn't too far from home." She looked around her nervously. "This place seems safe enough and I get tired being cooped up in the house. Robert doesn't want to go out much. Too much violence everywhere."

"Sounds like you've been watching too much TV, Judith. Hell, Cleveland's got more crime per capita than San Antonio. But you watch the local TV and read the newspaper and you'll think we're the worst place in the country." I let her hand drop. "There I go again, sounding like the Chamber of Commerce."

I looked around, saw her husband standing near the door. "Looks like your husband's about ready to leave."

She looked down at my belt and grinned. "I see you're still wearing your trademark, Paul. Or is it a brand?"

"It's just a belt buckle, ma'am. I don't really believe much in branding . . ."

She touched the seahorse, traced its edges and looked back up at me. "No?"

About that time, Margaret saw me talking with her and walked back over. When I introduced them, Judith smiled, "Oh, you're the one who bought the belt buckle for Paul."

Margaret wrapped her arm around me. "Stupid of me, wasn't it? But he wears it everywhere, even to the courthouse when he has a case."

"You're a lawyer?" Judith laughed. "I thought you were a rancher!" She had a good laugh, deep and a little husky, not the kind of laugh you'd expect from her handshake. She looked back up at me. "Robert's ready to go. Nice to see you again, Paul."

Okay, it's stupid, but I did start thinking the belt buckle was like a brand. 'Property of Margaret Ellis' it said so everyone I knew could see it. I stepped back a little, her arm falling away. "Time to go, sweetheart."

When we got back to her place, I looked at the rooms a little differently. Her paintings were hanging everywhere, cluttered, on chairs, all over the walls, little bits of Margaret whichever way I happened to look. When we made love, it felt almost mechanical, just another piece of Margaret's work. I almost expected her to sign my ass, on the bottom of my right cheek.

I didn't see Judith Johnson again for a few weeks and then bumped into her, literally, at the supermarket. My basket banged into hers when she turned the corner from the wine aisle.

When she saw who she'd hit, she said, "First my dog and then me! Paul Broller, what have you got against my family?"

"Shit, well, at least you didn't get killed from jumping in front of me. Your fault, ma'am. I was going straight down the lane and you turned and hit me. Any judge would find in my favor."

She closed her eyes for a moment, and I saw a faint blue shading her eyelids, nothing sparkly or cheap, just a taste of color added, hardly noticeable unless you were standing close to her. "Any Texas judge! If I had you in Ohio, though, I'd be wearing a neck brace and talking to my attorneys."

"Good thing we're in Texas, then. I'd hate to see that pretty neck of yours all wrapped up with a thick brace, ma'am." I don't know what it was about her that always pissed me off a little and made me drop into the cowboy mode, but she did. I'd have taken off my hat if I were wearing one. "What's your husband doing, Ms. Johnson? Still working on the fence?"

She worked her basket out of traffic and then

turned back to me. "No, he had to go back to Cleveland for a few days on business. The company has a small operation there, and Paul's being transferred back. We'll be moving again in two weeks."

I listened to her, but was mostly watching the way she moved, the front of my basket only a few inches away from her nicely rounded bottom. I did manage to make all the appropriate noises about how sorry I was that she and her husband were having to move again and asked what business her husband was in. I wasn't terribly surprised when she said, "Computers. He's a distributor for a company in Cleveland." I was stereotyping, but had an immediate picture of Robert Johnson with one of those little pocket protectors in his shirt pocket and computer screens reflected in his thick glasses. Not fair at all, I know, but there it is.

Sometimes things happen that really shouldn't happen and you even know they shouldn't but you go ahead anyway and let them happen. I'd known since Judith Johnson, dumb name, I wondered if she'd married him for the cute initials, had reached out and outlined that little seahorse on my belt buckle and I'd felt the slight pressure of her fingertips pushing it against my stomach that what I'd really like to do. Now I don't like myself when I feel this way, but what I'd really like to do was to reach out and muss up her perfect hair, just run my fingers all through it and uncurl that little wave under thing and make it all tangled and messy. I was thinking about that so much that my cart bumped right into her rear end when she came to a stop next to the hamburger section in the meat department.

"Sorry, Ms. Johnson." I laughed and pulled the cart back. "That was an accident, kind of day dreaming. Guess you'd better buckle your seat belt in this kind of traffic."

She gave me that stare again, the open eyes looking right into you kind of a stare. "That's called 'rear-ending,' Paul, and any judge, even in Texas, would find you guilty of reckless driving."

"Yes, ma'am, I'll just plead *nolo contendere* to the charge, your honor."

She had to have the last word, though. She lifted her head up, eyes still staring into mine, and said in what for a Texan would have been a very affected voice, but was her natural way of speaking, "The court finds you guilty, Mr. Broller. Your sentence is to follow me home, not too closely please, and help carry all this stuff in for me. I'll give you the rest of the sentence when we get there."

Her eyes flicked back down to that damned seahorse. "And watch out for Sebastian II!" She put a pound of hamburger with the rest of the stuff in her cart and wheeled it on down to the checkout line.

I followed her, three seconds behind, just like they teach in defensive driving school for people who get tickets and pulled my Bronco II into her driveway, parking it about two feet from her little Geo Prizm.

She loaded me down with three heavy bags of groceries and then seemed to take forever to find her housekey and get the door open. The new Sebastian barked, but he was out in the back yard, running free inside the new fence.

"Just put them down on the counter," she said. She was standing right in the pathway to the kitchen, so I had to brush up against her to get through. I managed to get all three bags down without dropping anything and then turned back around to leave.

"The second part of your sentence, Paul," she said, and she reached out and took my hand in hers, pulling it to her cheek, "is to do what you've had in mind since that first day you walked into my house and saw me." She turned her head slightly and just very softly kissed the palm of my hand.

Well, she was the judge and I was the condemned man and, in my professional life, an officer of the court, so I did what any man would have done under those circumstances. I pulled her into a real tight hug and then let my hands stroke her back and neck a little bit. She felt real good up against me like that. Then I did it. Moved my hands up and rubbed them all over her hair, tangling it all into a real mess so you couldn't even see that little perfect curl anymore. She looked a lot like one of those punk rock stars, but with black hair instead of orange or purple.

What I didn't expect was her reaction.

She just stood there for what must have been a full

minute, staring at me, and then a big old tear welled up in her eye and ran down over her cheek. I still think that was deliberate. Good actresses can make that happen almost like the rest of us can force a smile every once in a while.

"Damn that felt good," I said. "I've been wanting to do that since the first day we met."

That's when she started screaming at me. I won't repeat everything she said, but it sure didn't sound much like the Cleveland she'd been talking about since day one. Turned out I was an SOB, an unregenerate cowboy lawyer, a total failure as a man and several other things I just don't feel quite like repeating. I stood there and took it for a while and I guess I deserved it. She'd expected something else and some of us just don't like surprises very much.

Finally, when she'd wound down again and had started repeating herself and that took a good little while, believe me, I apologized. I'm still not sure I should have apologized but it's usually a good deal to say you're sorry when someone's real pissed off at you for something. And I guess I did feel a little guilty.

"Your turn," I said.

"What?"

"I did what I'd been wanting to do." I grinned sheepishly at her and started putting my fingers through my belt loops, a habit I have when I'm nervous. I never know what to do with my hands. "So, you can do what you've been wanting to do."

I didn't really like the look in her eyes when she hiccupped once and then walked over to me and knelt in front of me, but it felt pretty good when her hands slipped down just inside the waistband of my jeans. "How do you unbuckle this thing?" she asked.

I looked down at her and combed her hair with my fingers. "It's a western belt, Judith," I said. "It just pulls loose."

She managed to get it loose and pulled the belt all the way off. Then she stood up, turned around and walked into the kitchen. I followed her in and saw her fumble around in one of the drawers for a minute. I got a lot nervous when she pulled out a butcher's cleaver and held it up. It was real shiny, the light from the kitchen reflected off it and into my eyes.

"Hey, wait a minute! Damn it, wait!" I yelled at her, but she was just too ticked off to listen and then, THUNK! she banged the cleaver down and severed the buckle from the belt.

She looked up at me again and grinned. "I've wanted this damned sea horse for a long time, Paul. My friends in Cleveland will love it!"

A War Story

He didn't like war, but he knew war wasn't about liking or not liking. He had gone to war for his own not particularly good reasons. He could no longer even remember the reasons. He grew tired of people who always asked his reasons for going to war. War wasn't about reasons. He was not sure what war was really about, but he knew it was not about reasons.

He had sat on a hill once, surrounded by hundreds of other men, no women, that's just how things turned out, but there were women in the war, they just weren't sitting on the hill. While he was sitting on the hill, surrounded by all those men, he heard a thump and then another thump and then a series of quick thumps. After some of the thumps, he heard men screaming. Mostly they were screaming obscenities. And then the thumping sounds stopped.

A few minutes later, he found out that his unit had been attacked by the enemy. Mortars, just mortars. No one had fired a shot. No one had looked an enemy in the eye. *Glory*, he thought, glory. War is glorious. I have sat on a hill and I have been attacked by the enemy and I have survived to fight again. And so, he continued to sit on the hill. The sun rose and he saw dead men and living men, most of the men were among the living, only two were dead. Flies buzzed around the dead ones until a detail of men hauled them away in plastic bags.

He drank water from his canteen. He opened a can of rations and ate peaches. He smoked a cigarette. He had not smoked before going to war. He kept his eyes turned out to the perimeter. There might be an attack following the mortar attack. But there was no attack following the mortar attack, only helicopters buzzing around like flies.

A Day in the Life

Roger Alcutt walked down South Alamo Street. Not an uncommon occurrence in and of itself, but uncommon enough for Roger. Roger did not live in San Antonio, had never been in San Antonio and was not now in San Antonio. So, he was somewhat bewildered to find himself on a very dirty street filled with other people like him, people who really didn't belong there. Some of them asked others of them questions. How do I get to the Statue of Liberty? And other people, trying to look like natives, gave directions that would get them nowhere very quickly.

Roger stumbled on a crack in the old sidewalk just outside of a teahouse called Espuma and said "Excuse me!" when he stumbled into a young Chicana who had just come out of Chinoise/Chicana, a trendy new restaurant nowhere near the East Village. The crack in the sidewalk said, "damned right," and the young Chicana brushed on by. Roger looked down at the crack. "What did you say?" The crack stayed silent and the people around him began to edge slightly away.

"How do I get to Times Square?" a fat woman wearing only a thong asked him.

"I'm a stranger here myself," Roger murmured. "Sorry."

The fat woman hit him with her purse and pedaled her bicycle across the street. She descended into the dark mouth of the station to catch the crosstown train. As Roger looked, the mouth closed and he heard crunching sounds.

Everyone on the street except Roger wore bright checked Bermuda shorts and Tommy Bahama shirts. They looked like bright flowers blooming on the mostly gray street and spoke in various languages. From time to time, one would vanish into the station. Roger never saw anyone coming out.

One of several taxis stopped next to him and asked if he needed transportation. He could not figure out why they stopped unless it was maybe the pin-striped suit he was wearing. "*Hay demasiada coches*," he yelled. Immediately, seventy *migras* leaped out of the bushes and beat him senseless.

"*No soy de Mejico*!" he yelled. The biggest and fastest of *los federales* said "*No hablamos español*, dickhead," and kept beating him.

"*No trabajo a* Walmart," he wept. "*No quisiero trabajar aquí*!" But by then the San Antonio Chapter of the Republic of Texas *Federales* had poured him into the back of a blue and white.

Strip-searched and left in a wire cage in the back lot of a trailer park, Ricardo Arcuna (he had said that was not his name, but his green card told the truth) lay in the hot dust of the central San Antonio desert and cried, *"Dios mío! No me llamo 'Arcuna,' me llamo 'Alcutt.'"*

Later that night, coyotes howling from the Davis Mountains, a bitter wind woke him. *"Quien va a ayudarme?"* He looked up at the cold moon. His hands gripped the wire of his cage and pulled two strands almost apart. He pushed one hand through and the rest of his body followed, seeped out of the cage and into the crowded streets of Ciudad Acuna.

Almost naked, wearing only ripped jeans, skinny to the point of emaciation, he whispered, *"gracias"* when a man dropped a few pesos into his too large sombrero. He curled himself around the hat, head between his knees and dreamed of a life where he went to the office each day, had a beautiful blonde wife and children on the honor roll. Dreams much too strange for *el centro histórico*.

He stood up, naked in the hot sun, and walked north.

When he got to the Rio Bravo, he dove in. Gasping for breath, he surfaced and, sputtering, saw bombs falling on Baghdad. *"No sé,"* he whispered and dived back into the dirty water, *"no sé."*

"Get back in the ranks, troop!" a big man in a desert-camouflaged uniform screamed at him. "You miserable prick, move it, move, move, move!" He looked out across the desert, blowing sand forcing him to squint, and saw rank after rank of Bedouins on horseback. Each of them pointed directly at him, dug spurs into his horse or camel and launched Stinger missiles. *"Madre de Dios!"* he screamed. Ricardo closed his eyes and clicked his jungle boot heels together three times, but when he opened them, he was still somewhere near the Tigris River.

He felt hot, his uniform burning. Flames engulfed him and he sank into the Tigris, still burning even in the dirty water of the river. Burning. His clothes charred, turned to ashes, he sank naked into the water. When his boots touched bottom, he looked up and ascended, one slow inch at a time until he saw the roof of the river, the bottom of the sky. A giant hand pushed down on his head. Then he saw nothing at all.

What Art Needs

El arte necesita generar el espacio del individuo percibiendo el tiempo.
  –Gabriel Orozco in *Letras /Libres*. D.F., Mexico, January 2004.

A lbert Montague does not care much what the police think. He walks down the much-in-need-of-sweeping street in central San Antonio without even considering the police or the law or what people love to call "property rights." He has been looking at photos by Gabriel Orozco, the great Mexican photographer and essayist, and his imagination has been seized. "Yes, seized," he whispers. He mumbles as he walks, "Art needs to create a space . . ." "Space needs to be created for art . . ."

His Spanish is not very good. What does Orozco mean by "perceive the time?" Does *percibiendo* even mean *perceive*? I think so, he thinks. I could consult my Velasquez but it's in my office, an office, the office that I go to when I have the need to create a living instead of live for creating. "The time?" What does he mean? "A busted soccer ball, smashed, water filling the indentation, a space for art, for the casual observer, no, for the non casual observer." He spits in a dirty brown colored puddle and the gob of spit sends ripples, very gentle, slow-moving, large enough to capsize a small piece of paper that has been carrying two ants. "A space, time . . ."

He veers into the center of the street. He deliberately creates a space as cars swerve around him. He looks straight ahead. "Individual perception." "Each person, surely he is speaking only of artists, perceives something." "Perceives art and creates a space to see it in time."

Nuestra memoria y nuestro olvido son más importantes que el clima o la manufactura de una obra para ser conservada en la historia.
                                            –Gabriel Orozco

And so, Albert says to himself, no one else is paying attention, "it's all up to our memories and our forgetfulness, without memory, no art. But why forgetfulness? That is what *olvido* means, isn't it? That doesn't make sense."

The street comes to a dead end and he turns onto Commerce Street. He looks up at an extremely tall statue that seems to twine in its redness until it forms almost a yin yang symbol at its top. "Crap," he says. "And occupying so much space."

"The Torch of Friendship." That's what Consul Castañeda had called the statue by Sebastian. "May it always stand tall to symbolize the ties of friendship that forever bind our countries," he had said.

Albert remembers Ozzie Osborne at the Alamo. "He marked the space," he mutters. He circles the statue. "What would Orozco say? What would he photograph if he were here?" He drops his pants and pisses on the base of the towering red monument. "Piss, perceive, conceive for the pullulating mobs," he screams. And when he looks down at the base of the shiny red statue, he sees the small pool of yellow widen, stretch out, run down into a gutter. "Art," he smiles.

El arte crece como crece el universo. Y el universo se está expandiendo en todas direcciones.

He loves Orozco, loves the pale blue ball sitting in the rainy gray street. "Art creates as the universe was created." He has a feeling he has gotten something wrong. "And the universe expands in all directions" "Creating its own time?" he wonders. "Why the blue ball? Only one. Why the smashed soccer ball? Only one."

Albert Montague feels he is thinking great thoughts

as he wanders back into the street. So many round things and Orozco says he is not interested in composition and the composition makes the photos great.

He walks straight down the middle of the street to the Blue Star Art Space but cannot remember what he has planned to do there. His happening is over; he has no more piss to give. He jots a quick note on a piece of paper he finds in the middle of the street. It is only a brief sentence he has memorized:

Una caja de zapatos es una caja de zapatos, antes, durante y después de la exposición.

"Before, during and after," he mutters and throws himself under the wheels of a Lone Star Beer truck.

For a space, for a brief time, Albert Montague's shoe is displayed at the Blue Star. For that was the last sentence, his last request, he wrote on the piece of paper he found.

Strung Out in Suburbia

ne eye on a dark night, car moving slowly down the highway, one headlight not burning, dark. Two boys inside: one 16, one just turned 17. Cops spot the missing headlight and stop the car, not cops, sheriff's department with dogs to sniff. Sheer terror in their faces, the boys huddled inside.

Interim: That highway, U.S. 77, from South Padre Island to Corpus Christi stretches through the King Ranch, runs, when it passes Padre Island and Brownsville, alongside the Rio Grande. Migrant workers stream across the border, checkpoints strategically located, invasion also of killer bees, Africanized honeybees, traps set for insects and young men and women. Boring blacktop, desolate landscape that Eddie Johnston has driven so many times.

The other eye at home, waiting, not knowing what has happened. First call (10 p.m.): "On the way home. Sorry, dad, I should never have left for the Island. I fucked up royally. Be home in a few hours." Relief, new worry. Eddie places the phone carefully in its cradle. He tells Elizabeth that Danny is safe. They have worried for two nights because he had left home without telling them. Now they worry again, late night driving, exhaustion, spring break. The radio has warned recently that the second greatest cause of car accidents is Driving While Exhausted, DWE, a new acronym.

But they have never expected this. A second call at 11 p.m., this one from the Kleberg County jail. "Sorry, sir, but we've just arrested your son. POCS (possession of a controlled substance) not less than one, no more than four grams. He's 17, an adult, 2nd or 3rd degree felony. XTC, Ecstasy, we think. It's in the lab." Doom drug. He tells Elizabeth.

Eddie Johnston hugs Elizabeth close. When he closes his eyes he can almost see his son in the sheriff's car, late at night, strung out, too much beach, too many drugs, in handcuffs. He and Elizabeth had not known their son used drugs, can't help looking back over the past year, blame themselves for what they can now see as classic signs. When he is not blaming himself, Eddie pictures Danny wearing old jeans, granny glasses, Docs on his feet with dirty white socks. He is sitting in the back seat of the sheriff's car, hands cuffed behind his back. Not a minor at 17, not in Texas.

The deputy who had called told Eddie that. Tomorrow, he will find out that Danny was strip searched, thrown in jail to spend the night, throwing up, scared shitless, his friend, one month younger, sixteen, driven 40 miles away to juvenile detention, car impounded. Danny lies on a thin pallet on a dirty cot, thinks it's all rotten luck, yes, luck that landed him where he is, luck that his birthday was a month earlier, that he is no longer a juvenile. He cries, sleeps fitfully to awaken to a new kind of reality.

1

Eddie and Elizabeth telephone anyone they think can help: friends with connections, attorneys they know, people referred to them by people they know. *What should I do?* Eddie wonders. *How do I find a good attorney in Kleberg County?* He does not feel alive, forces himself to breathe in and out. He has never done anything more difficult than breathing, has to focus on drawing air in and pushing it out, heaving gasps. On the seventh call, he gets the name of an attorney, will check him out later, find out the network has paid off, an old network of friends and friends of friends leading to the best lawyer in the county.

3 a.m. and a hundred phone calls later: No sleep. A mad dash to all night grocery stores trying to cash

checks. Eddie gets money at seven different conven-
ience stores, all with low limits after midnight. He and
Elizabeth get in his car, an aging Bronco II, and turn
on to IH-37 headed south towards Corpus Christi,
drinking Diet Cokes and coffee. He does not normally
drink coffee. He fights to stay awake, tries to stay alert.
They stop frequently to refuel. He is smoking again
after a year away from tobacco, chain smoking, his
own narcotic, and drinking Diet Coke after Diet Coke.
Elizabeth does not complain.

Three hours later, they reach the outskirts of
Corpus. Eddie sees the sun rise over the northern
suburbs of the city and turns west on Highway 77 to
Kingsville, county seat of Kleberg County, a small
town on the road to South Padre Island where tens of
thousands of students party every day and night. He
cannot see the bay or the gulf, thinks of a time two
years earlier canoeing the bay with his son, fishing,
catching speckled trout and paddling. He almost falls
asleep, jerks himself awake. Elizabeth is still awake,
has cried almost steadily for three hours. He rests his
hand on her thigh, squeezes reassuringly. She slips her
hand in his.

*Interim: Something has happened to Eddie's son.
Something he cannot protect him from. He asks
himself why he hadn't seen it earlier, blames the fire
that burned Danny's room to the ground five weeks
earlier, blames himself, blames the high school. He*

126

*cannot breathe, is consumed with anger at every-
thing, even his son, especially his son, especially himself, essentially himself. He drives south and then
west.*

As Eddie drives, scenes he has never seen play
themselves out in his mind: Danny Johnston is
booked, fingerprinted, thrown into a cell. One of his
three cellmates, Eddie will find out this afternoon, is
a convicted child molester, but Danny is no longer a
child. Eddie can almost see him: sunburned, thin,
strung out, shivering on a thin mattress on a steel cot,
can see a toilet and sink, stark, open, can see the cot
above him sagging with the weight of his cellmate. He
sees his son shiver, cry, fall restlessly asleep to wake
up vomiting, emptying his stomach on the floor and
then in the open toilet, reaction to the drug, not
Ecstasy but Wig, XTC plus.

At 8 a.m., a cloudy day in the normally hot and
sunny weather of Kingsville, Texas, Eddie and Elizabeth Johnston wait, holding hands quietly, in the
doorway of Howard Suarez, the best lawyer in Kleberg
County. He shows them in. They sit on a cushioned
leather sofa, look up at the mounted heads of four deer
and a javelina, explain why they're there. The lawyer
says, "Wait here." He goes to the courthouse and
arranges bond. Eddie writes a check for $1,000, 10%
of a $10,000 PA bond. They will meet their son at
11:30 a.m. after he has been magistrated. Such a long,

long day! But they still have "Pretrial Services" to visit with their son.

At 9 a.m., Eddie Johnston stands with his wife in front of the Kleberg County Courthouse. The jail occupies the top two floors. He looks up at the barred windows wishing he was inside and Danny was here on the sidewalk. *Nothing in my life*, he thinks, *will ever be harder than this. Nothing ever will be.*

At 11:30 a.m., they see Danny for the first time since Monday morning. He is skinny, dirty, sunburned. His blonde hair almost bleached against the red of his skin, his eyes puffy. He is wearing old clothes and a new orange bracelet that identifies him as a prisoner in the Kleberg County Jail. He looks sullen, about to break. Eddie almost falls over, exhausted, crying, reaches out and touches his shoulder, makes contact for a moment. He had been wrong. This is worse. Elizabeth sits next to Danny and holds him.

They still have to wait for Pretrial Services to open at 1 p.m. They climb into the Bronco, Danny's orange bracelet can't be taken off yet, and drive out the highway to a Denny's, get drinks and smoke. Eddie and Danny smoke, almost a ritual, something they have never done together, something Eddie had never permitted his son to do in his presence.

After coffee, they drive back to the courthouse and walk to the Adult Probation building where Pre-Trial Services is located. Elizabeth is exhausted, can barely walk. The building is filled with people Eddie considers children, but who are legally adults, and a few older men. Very few speak English. Eddie discovers that this is also the parole reporting center.

Danny tells him that one of the bad things the night before was that no one in his cell spoke English. He does not speak Spanish, takes third-year honors French in high school. He had been so alone in there. Rationally, Eddie think that's good, that maybe it will help. What Danny has left is the fear, only the fear. If he fucks up once more, he knows, the cops have reinforced this, he is back in Kleburg County, back in the jail. The fear, Eddie thinks, has got to see him through, work with him.

All the young men in the office are Hispanic, only Danny an Anglo. Most of the caseworkers are women in their twenties or early thirties, all but one an Anglo. Cocky, leering at the probation counselors, the probationers say things in a language Eddie can not understand, but the body language is clear, insolent, bravado, young men strutting, hips thrust out. Danny is taken away again, fills out papers, has a urinalysis, the first of dozens still to come.

He is given a calendar of events, the next urinalysis, the arraignment date, his restrictions.

Eddie cannot stop crying unless he retreats into a still, emotionless place with no feelings whatsoever. He finds that place, knows it is dangerous to retreat into such a place for overlong, but the coldness stops the tears, and he cannot help his son if he dissolves into tears.

That afternoon, they get back in the car, stop for a sandwich. Danny throws his up, leaning out of the car on the side of Highway 77 heading east, heading away from the beach, away from Kleburg County, leaving remnants of an Arby's roast beef with cheese on the shoulder of the highway. Eddie is terrified, does not know what to say. He does not know the young punk in the back seat who sometimes has to lean out of the car door and vomit. Knowing, like trust, will take time and patience and support. The love will always be there. Finally, Danny falls asleep, Elizabeth dozes fitfully, and Eddie drives back home, 300 more miles, home.

Danny's room is still being repaired, no bed, no floor covering, workers still taping and floating. He will sleep in the study, when he can sleep.

2

That first night home Duane visits. He is Danny's friend, a friend who has been through it before, has been hospitalized and is in recovery. He acts like an AA sponsor. He is Christ. He is so young. Eddie needs his help with Danny, but cannot jeopardize his recovery. Duane has bought the whole 12-step program; Danny cannot buy the God part of it, resists a leap of faith that seems a basic requirement for any 12-step program. They sit late at night crying together, talking. Danny is still throwing up, Wig, worse than XTC, dreamed up in a lab in Austin, keeps his stomach in turmoil.

Duane holds him, comforts him, they comfort each other, then he leaves and Danny and Eddie go to whatever it is that isn't sleep but resembles it.

The next day Eddie makes arrangements, not easy. Workers tromp through the house, rebuilding from the fire, moving through their lives. Danny is still strung out, on the edge, his stomach continuing to reject food. They have both cried all night. Eddie has screened phone calls, reminds himself to change the phone number and make it unlisted. He does not go to work. Elizabeth is sick, her worry gnawing at her.

Danny is still on spring break. The family doctor recommends Emetrol to help with the vomiting, schedules them for a visit that afternoon with the Alamo Mental Health Spectrum Center, the Spectrum Chemical Dependency Program. They arrive for the appointment at 4 p.m. and meet with Joyce, the family counselor who will be the assessment counselor for Danny. They chat for one hour, and she checks him into the hospital for detox and rest.

Eddie has had a total of six hours of sleep over a 72-hour period and still cannot sleep. He and Elizabeth get home, both totally trashed. They hug each other constantly, the tears starting to dry up, still not really believing, lie in the bed staring at the ceiling. They wonder what they did wrong as parents, why they hadn't noticed a drug problem earlier. The next morning, they do not go to work. They go to the hospital, stay with Danny as long as they can. He is in pain, does not want to be in the hospital.

Interim: The law. By Texas law, Danny is an adult at age 17. That means several things: 1) he will be tried as an adult, 2) he has the authority to make decisions for himself, and, oddly, 3) his parents are responsible for those decisions. Danny can, if he likes, sign himself out of the hospital, something he threatens to do several times. He actually signs the papers on four different occasions and then withdraws them. What keeps him in the hospital is that he knows he will go back to jail if he is not in a treatment program. He does not think he is addicted to anything. He may not, in fact, be chemically addicted. He is, though, addicted socially. There's a difference.

Danny's best friend, a bright boy named Jonathan, returns from his spring break trip to Cancun the next day. Danny and Jonathan have been in the gifted and talented program and met in their first classes in high school, though Jonathan is a senior and Danny is officially a junior. "Danny and I are brothers," he says. "I'll do anything for him. I thought he was dead." Jonathan cries.

"Will you turn yourself in for treatment? Not to the cops, just check yourself in for rehab?" Eddie asks. "Your father's insurance will pay for it. Do you care that much for Danny?"

Jonathan says. "I am so sad. I am always sad. Danny and I understand each other, do everything together, even Wig. But we can stop like that!" He snaps his fingers. "There are two kinds of people in the world," he says. "The people who blow a little grass and the drinkers."

"Danny is going to jail," Eddie says, "if he flunks even one urinalysis in the next two years. I can't let you near him if you're going to do things that will get him back in trouble, even smoking grass."

"I'll stop," he says. "But no treatment. I don't need it."

That night, Jonathan visits Danny. He smuggles in a pack of cigarettes, tells Danny he's strong, has the will power to stop without staying in the hospital. Danny agrees. Eddie sits with them a minute and hears his son agreeing with Jonathan and he does something he has never done before. He takes Jonathan's hand in his, retreats to that cold, empty space, and says, "If you continue this, even if you are not around when Danny falls, I will track you down like an animal and I will kill you myself."

Jonathan looks blankly at him. "I learned how in Vietnam. If you do anything that hurts Danny, if you are even around and he starts to smoke, I swear to you that I will find you and you will die." Eddie stands up and walks away.

If he had the authority, Eddie would insist that Jonathan be banned from visiting Danny in the hospital, but he has no authority, only responsibility. Jonathan stops and wants to talk to him as he leaves, but Eddie has not emerged from that cold place and Jonathan sees nothing but ice in his eyes. He knows that Eddie will, in fact, kill him if he harms Danny. Danny says he is going to sign out, go live with Jonathan for a few days until he has his head on straight.

Eddie tells him he will call the police and report Jonathan as a drug abuser, that he will call Jonathan's mother and tell her, that he will have a group meeting of every parent of every friend Jonathan and Danny have had for the last year and discuss their sons' and daughters' drug problems.

Jonathan pulls Danny aside, glances at Eddie and whispers to him. Eddie grins at Jonathan, his eyes remain cold. Jonathan says, "It's cool, man. I'll be back." Danny does not sign out, but it is not Eddie's threats, it is the fear of going back to jail.

3

Hospital nights blend into one long night. Danny cannot leave unless he leaves all the way, signs himself out, goes to jail in Kingsville. He does not, will not sign himself out. When Elizabeth and Eddie visit, they take

Danny out to the patio, talk about what has happened and why it has happened.

Danny and Eddie always light up, the smoke moving between them, Elizabeth sits, not smoking but joining in the conversation. Eddie fools himself into thinking the smoke ritual is important, binding. At family group the night before, Danny had said, "There's a real bond between my dad and me. We like a lot of the same things."

Eddie wonders about that, agrees, but is troubled. He can remember when Danny had asked, during a late evening drive returning from a three-day visit to relatives in Chicago, whether he had ever done grass or anything in the 60s. He had told him that, yes, he had smoked grass, had experimented with LSD, mescaline, psylocibin during the 60s. But had stopped after the experiments, can still count on the fingers of one hand the number of times he had taken psychotropic drugs and, besides, he had been older. The first time he had smoked grass, he said, had been in Vietnam and, when he was 25 years old, back from the war and in graduate school on a very few occasions he had dropped psychedelics just to see what it was like. He had not done it often, had never liked the feeling of being out of control and unable to stop when he wanted to.

So what can he say now? "I did it. You can't. What you've done is wrong." He cannot be hypocritical with his son. He does wish, though, that he had never said anything. That he had just kept his mouth shut. There is a bond, a truth they have always spoken with each other, to each other.

He remembers when Danny had asked him if he had ever killed anyone in the war. He had first answered no and then told him that he wanted to be honest with him, that there had been a time, even though he had not pulled the trigger himself. "While I was in Dak To," he had told Danny then, "I listened to a young boy report on convoys leaving the camp. His reports were probably the signal for the Viet Cong to prepare their ambushes. I got to know him on my radio. He called himself "Bao" and sounded about sixteen years old, about your age. I translated his words for two weeks, then DFed him and, as he began his broadcast one morning, signaled the base Ops Officer. I watched from the front of my tent as our planes strafed his hill and dropped bombs on him. He was that close to the base. I flinched as I saw American planes sow napalm seeds that flowered, bursting into red blossoms against the green of dark hills. Early one morning in the war. I didn't pull the trigger myself," he had said, "but I never heard Bao again. I was not a combat soldier."

Eddie thinks that at that time Bao must have been about the same age as Danny is now, and he listens as Danny says "I can stop all of it, will stop all of it, but grass should be legal." He hasn't harmed anyone. Even the Wig was just him and his friends; no one else got hurt. "You got hurt, Danny," Eddie says. "Don't ever forget how you were that night in jail. Don't ever forget how you were heaving your guts out in the car on the way home. Don't ever forget that if you make one slip, flunk one urinalysis, you are back for a minimum of two years in the Kleburg County Jail. And, if someone asks, don't even think about arguing for legalization."

He's done it. He has told his son to lie. In spite of everything, Danny is one of the brightest, most intelligent and honest people he has ever met.

After five days and nights in the hospital, Danny is scheduled to move to intensive outpatient treatment for six months. He will graduate from high school at the "special" school for CD kids, though his diploma will have the name of the school he has attended for the past three years. Eddie loves all the new acronyms. "CD" has always meant "Certificate of Deposit" or "Compact Disk," but now he knows a third meaning, one he really wishes he had never learned, "chemically dependent." Danny will attend CD groups every morning and work on his classes in the afternoons. But Elizabeth and Eddie's major concern now is that Danny will be coming home for the evenings.

That past weekend, he and Susan had attended their first Al-Anon meeting and had felt out of place among the family members of alcoholics. They had been the only parents of a CD kid and had detected what almost seemed to be a weird kind of fierce pride among the Al-Anon members, almost as if each tried to outdo the previous speaker.

Interim: They have learned a lot about AA in the past week. They have spoken with therapists, case workers, counselors. Each has recommended that they attend Al-Anon meetings. Alcoholics Anonymous developed the first major Twelve-Step Program for recovering alcoholics and it has worked for thousands of chemically dependent alcohol abusers. Al-Anon, for families of alcoholics, and Narc-Anon, an AA lookalike for drug addicts, use the same twelve-step program developed by AA. Eddie confesses that he is cynical about the whole program, though, mostly about its reliance on a caring God. Each step of the program is a pledge to put your lives in God's hands. He read the underlying message that he is responsible for his own life, that his son must take responsibility for his. From the first moment, when he said, "Hi, my name is Eddie" and 47 other people said, "Hi, Eddie," in chorus, he has been unable to avoid the cynicism that creeps into his mind. The structure works, obviously, but it seems all structure without a deep faith. Danny, he knows and almost regrets, has inherited that cynical streak.

That first night Danny comes home, they rent a video. Eddie forgets what it was; it's not important.

Elizabeth cooks Stephen's favorite food. By coincidence, the homily at mass the previous Sunday had been on the text of the parable of the prodigal son and Eddie laughs out loud in the middle of the homily. But they are doing the whole prodigal son bit now, everything, but with meatballs instead of a fatted calf.

Late that night Danny and Eddie sit under one of the tall ash trees in the back yard. Cigarette smoke drifts upward and they drink sodas. Danny's random urinalysis would detect even a trace of alcohol and his pre-trial supervision and personal appearance bond would be broken.

"I've got a problem, Dad," he says, and sits quietly until Eddie looks up.

"That I know!" Eddie stands up and walks back toward the alley, inhaling deeply and then flicks the butt over the cedar fence.

"No, not that. I owe a guy three hundred dollars for the stuff I took down to Padre Island."

Eddie doesn't want to hear, stares out into the alley, the floodlights in the neighbors' back yards cast three versions of his shadow backwards in the too tall grass. "Three hundred dollars?"

"Yes, a group of us went in on the buy. Fifteen dollars a pill, but they would have cost twenty dollars each if we'd bought them separately."

"You mean you were dealing?" He stares at his son, clenches his fists, sees the darkest of his three shadows cover Danny's face.

"No, not dealing. I wasn't going to make any money from it. It's just that one of us had to actually make the buy, and Jonathan was going to Cancun. Berto, I don't know his last name, fronted the stuff for me, some of the guys didn't have the cash when I made the buy, and Jonathan says he's getting antsy for his money."

"Shit." He sits back down. It is all really too much. "You know your mom's having to have counseling, don't you? That costs a lot of money."

"I'm sorry, Dad, really. But I have to give the guy three hundred dollars."

Later that night, they climb into Eddie's Bronco II and drive out of the neighborhood. Eddie is more than a little frightened. He is driving late at night to make half, that's all he'll pay, of a three hundred dollar payment to a two-bit dealer. It reminds him of a convoy he had been on, very short, from the base camp down to the town of Dak To. There was nothing really dangerous about the convoy, but in the dark, he knew, anything could happen. He knows, now, that he is breaking the law by helping Danny deliver the cash, but he can't find a way out.

He slows down, turns into an adjacent suburb, passes the house. The house belongs to one of the teachers at Danny's old school. Her daughter, according to Danny, dates Berto, and she delivers orders of grass and other drugs as needed and collects money from the other kids at school. Berto is 26. She is 16. Danny says she frequently shows up at school bruised. Eddie is afraid the house is being watched. It has been that kind of week. He drives by the house slowly, looking everywhere in the dark, but can't see any suspicious cars. He circles back and pulls the car to the right side of the street, tell his son to roll down the window. He close his eyes for a moment as Danny opens the mailbox door and slips the cash inside. Then, he pulls forward, drives the few blocks back home.

"Call her and tell her the money's in the mailbox, half of it, and that she needs to get it out right away. Tell her your mom and dad busted you, flushed everything down the toilet, that that's all the money you were able to collect before we put you in a rehab center." He turns away. "I'm going to bed."

4

A week later, they all drive down to Kingsville to make a show of family solidarity.

Danny has been scheduled for arraignment. The drive is not like the last time, not so late at night. Everyone is tense, but all of the crying has stopped. The miles race past and Eddie turns back onto highway 77 circling Corpus Christi to make the hot drive west past the King Ranch and into Kleberg County.

For the past few weeks, they have been going to

group sessions at the hospital. Danny has talked about his life, his sexual habits, his inner secrets with Eddie and Elizabeth and a therapist he has never met before and has also been going to CD groups. *The family that groups together stays together*, Eddie thinks. It all seems like some kind of fantastic put on. And they have also had regular family meetings to discuss their progress, almost all of those leading to more tension. After each group session or family meeting, they have all felt worse than they felt before, have almost outdone each other, being more open and honest than the one who spoke before, just the three of them, communicating.

Communication sucks, Eddie thinks. *Kleburg County sucks. Everything sucks.*

Still, the very worst of the group sessions are not those that involve just his family and a counselor. The worst are those sessions when groups of families get together. Those sessions become open invitations for the kids to insult the parents. Parents wind up having their nerves shredded as their teenagers rip into them. One of the boys calls his mother a bitch and a whore. "I hate her," he says. She sits there weeping openly. The counselor offers pabulum, words like "Now, Johnny has to get his issues out. We all need to be brutally honest."

What Danny says is mild compared to the others. The "in family" sessions were, if he had to sum them up, mildly helpful. The multi-family sessions were so abrasive on the nerves of the parents that they seemed destructive. The other possibility, Eddie knows, is that they have simply had a very bad counselor as session leader.

Kingsville isn't a very large town. The courthouse is red brick with white decorative brick on the corners. In the tradition of smaller Texas towns, the courthouse occupies a whole block with streets radiating out from it making a classic town square. *Lots of lawyers*, Eddie thinks, as they park the car and walk down the street to their lawyer's office.

Danny wears a shiny new suit, and his hair is freshly cut short. His shoes are polished to a high sheen, but the Kingsville dust has already coated them. When Eddie pushes the door open to the lawyer's office, Sonya, his legal secretary looks up. "Can I help you?"

"Yes, we have a court date today, an arraignment. Is Mr. Suarez in?"

"Felony or misdemeanor?"

"Felony, why?"

"Well, misdemeanors are normally held in the morning. Arraignments for felonies don't normally begin until 1:30. But Mr. Suarez won't be back until 3. He's giving a speech in Corpus."

"He's my son's lawyer. Eddie says. "Why isn't he here?"

"Just a minute," Sonya says. "I'll check. If he were

supposed to be in court with you, he'd be here."

He gives her Danny's Pre-Trial Supervision papers. According to the papers, he is supposed to be arraigned today, then go to the parole building and pee in a bottle to prove he hasn't been using.

Sonya calls the courthouse. "We'll get Mr. Suarez back if he's supposed to be there," she says. She talks for a few minutes about Danny and court dates, then hangs up the phone. "No, his arraignment isn't for another two weeks. Someone got it wrong on the document they gave you."

When they walk back outside, the wind has picked up, blowing litter through the streets. The sun is still hot, burning down on them. Eddie unlocks the car. "It's still Office Visit Day at Pre-Trial Services. You have to go do the urinalysis," he tells Danny.

On the drive back to San Antonio, Elizabeth and Danny sleep. Eddie smokes and again considers giving up cigarettes.

Interim: Memory
His mind switches into that place where the car drives itself, his awareness no longer on the highway. It is three o'clock on a very hot day, but he is in the hospital, early one morning seventeen years ago. He has been there for 30 hours as Elizabeth has been straining with back labor and the fetal monitor has been squawking and beeping regularly. His hands are tired from massaging her back, but he knows her own aching is far worse than his. He drifts in and out of what he's doing, feels contractions grow inside her. Danny is kicking and turning getting ready for the

rough ride out to freedom. *When her water breaks*, a fantastic image water breaking, *he thinks, she soaks the entire bed, drips with liquid, warm and then cold. He buzzes for a nurse, waits five minutes and then storms out of the small room to the nurse's station. It is bad enough that Elizabeth has to go through all this, no need for her to have to be wet and cold at the same time.*

They wheel her into the delivery room just as the contractions begin to come more wildly, more unpredictably. In what the nurses call "transition," she pants, writhing on the gurney and lets herself be moved onto the delivery table. "Just a few more minutes, Elizabeth," the doctor says. "Hold her, Eddie, her hands." He holds her hands and feels the strength of them clasping him, hurting him, he had not known she had such strength, each time a new contraction rips through her. "Push, Elizabeth," the doctor says and she pushes, groans, her head rising from the pillow, her whole stomach tensing as the muscles gather to expel Danny.

"Just another few like that and he'll be here," the doctor says. "Come around here, Eddie. You can see his head crowning." And he moves from the head of the bed to the foot, bends down next to the doctor, sees a froth of yellow piss, green fluids and the red of Elizabeth's blood as her thighs tighten and she braces herself to push once more. "Here, put your hands right here."

He moves between Elizabeth's thighs, his eyes fastened on the swirling pastel of liquid color on Danny's hair, already blond, but bathed in running reds and greens. He sees Danny move, blinks his eyes, rubs his son's forehead, feels the warm liquids pouring from Elizabeth's vagina, sees the nose emerge, the closed eyes, the mouth all set to cry and scream and almost loses it all as Danny slips into his hands, his arms, all wet and sticky, his legs kicking already against whatever is waiting. He holds his son as the umbilical cord pulses, can hardly see anything but the small naked bundle in his arms. He walks over to Elizabeth, Danny in his arms. "Look what you did," he says, "what we did."

The doctor cuts the cord. He takes Danny and wipes the mucous from his nose, holds him up, crying, no need for the whap on the bottom. An antiseptic nurse, all in white, suctions his nose, does some things. Danny has passed his first test: a perfect score on something called an APGAR.

Eddie pulls into the driveway, pushes the button to open the garage. Danny and Elizabeth wake up. Another day. Only seventeen years after that other morning.

H. Palmer Hall's last book, *Foreign and Domestic*, is a collection of poems published by Turning Point Press in Cincinnati. His poetry, essays and poems have appeared in numerous literary magazines and anthologies, including *North American Review*, *Connecticut Review*, *The Texas Observer*, *Florida Review*, *Briar Cliff Review* and many others. He grew up in and around the Big Thicket of Southeast Texas where many of these stories are set. The library director at St. Mary's University, he currently lives in San Antonio, Texas, where he also serves as the editor of Pecan Grove Press.

www.ingramcontent.com/pod-product-compliance
Lightning Source LLC
Chambersburg PA
CBHW052138170626
46812CB00004B/1490